*Short Stories*

*for*

*The Most Famous Generation*

This is a work of fiction. Names, characters, businesses, organizations, places, events, and incidents are either the product of the author's imagination or are used fictitiously.

Any resemblance to actual persons, living or dead, events or locales is coincidental.

Copyright 2020 by Debbie Fowler

Revised 2025

All rights reserved

No unauthorized usage without permission of the author.

ISBN 9798692618290

Dedicated to the millions born

1946-1964


The Most Famous Generation does **not**
go quietly into that good night

It would be a mission impossible to choose a poster child for the Baby Boomer Generation. It *is* true that back in our salad days, we appeared virtually indistinguishable one from another, but young'uns habitually think they should attempt to be a mirror image to their peers, so in this regard we are not a unique species. But surely The Most Famous Generation has seen more choices that opened up and heaved themselves upon us in the years leading up to and following our initiation into the Wide World of Responsible Adulthood than most other demographic groups. So here is our distinction: those of us who experienced *our* chaotic wonder years during the 50's, 60's, and 70's have unique perspectives on values, challenges and the stuff of life. These viewpoints are unquestionably different from those of our predecessors and successors – whether better or worse I'll have to leave for others to say, but at the very least, distinct. Now we are knock, knock, knocking on the door to our golden years, and unavoidably, bittersweetly undergoing that post mid-life thing, a life-stage that *nobody* could have foreseen. The updates to technology, science, discoveries, fears, possibilities, and the horrific year 2020 would have made creative noggins like H.G. Wells, Tom Clancy, Gene Roddenberry, and L Frank Baum spin. To quote Gomer Pyle, "Sha-zam and Gaw-aw-ly!"

In my fifties, a lot of these perspectives began to romp through what's left of my mental faculty. One way I have found to deal with these unbidden, rowdy thoughts and feelings is to write them down and fling them out into the public arena. Of course, this exercise will not solve the puzzles of life, will not accomplish world peace, may not even light one candle in the darkness. But set aside all those noble goals, and maybe we can have a chuckle or two and some fond remembrances, opine about modern life and prepare some thoughts for impending Dinosaurhood. I'm certain that we Boomers have *not* left the building as yet, and can be counted on to articulate, contemplate, move and shake, yadda yadda yadda until they pry the reins from our cold dead fingers. This, even though some of the Millennials have coined a childishly harsh attitude toward us with the "Okay, Boomer" phenomenon. ("Why, when I was your age ...")

A thousand years ago (or was it just a couple of weeks?) when our grade school teachers asked us to calculate the age we would reach by the turn of the century (someone along the way gave it a glow-up with *The New Millennium*), we certainly expected that we'd be living like the Jetsons, and in many ways we *are* there. (Except, those way-cool flying cars are very very tardy!) But for the most part, retirement age is a big surprise to those of us who were advised by our teen-aged peers to be suspicious of anyone over the age of thirty. Since there is much remembering, observing and forecasting to do, I offer both comments and made-up stuff from my brain to honor a place/sense/study of yesterday, today, and tomorrow – a unique place in space and time called . . . *The Boomer Zone.*

# Chasing Erma Bombeck

*Baby steps into writing ... lonnnnnng ago and faaaaaar away.*
*This piece was published in*
<u>*Still Crazy Literary Magazine*</u>*.*

I can't remember not being a reader. Visits to the public library in my 1950/60s' childhood were as routine for my sister and me as trips to school and church. The required reading in high school was not as enjoyable as was the extracurricular, but I had little trouble with it – it was still reading, after all.

Writing, however, was something that other people did – born writers who must have known by the age of 3 that they would grow up to be prolific or provocative authors. I dutifully produced the assigned essays and compositions for English classes, and I received compliments on a couple of my efforts, but didn't choose to hear in those remarks any encouragement to point my goals toward anything bookish.

So I went on to live an ordinary, non-authorly life. I had a family, and most of my paying day jobs required little imagination beyond decisions about what outfit to wear. I continued to be a reader of many books, but creative writing remained as foreign a concept to me as quantum theory, Wall Street, current politics or Rap music.

But there came a time when I woke up to discover an inalienable truth – I had somehow passed Middle Age and was entering Use It or Lose It Territory. Up ahead on the horizon loomed Coulda Shoulda Woulda-ville and just prior to THE EPILOGUE, "Thanks for playing, we have some lovely parting gifts for you." All that newly raised consciousness overlapped the delivery of my very first personal computer. And the rest, as they say, is now in the rear-view mirror.

I timidly took a few baby steps once I'd familiarized myself with the word processing program on the new-fangled computer, thankfully forgiving and user-friendly. No white correction fluid, error-covering tape or wadded up balls of angst-filled paper as seen on TV in the offices of writers. I received nice feedback on a nostalgia piece I submitted to a local newspaper and further encouragement on a series of travel letters I sent back home electronically from a brief, serendipitous chance to work while traveling. I allowed wavy-edged visions of a 21$^{st}$ Century Erma Bombeck-esque career.

Pumped up, I speed-shifted from first into third gear. I self-published a non-fiction book and then a novel, began not one but three more books, wrote countless essays in the Erma style, and ventured into the short story. I joined a local writer's group and I receive encouragement from my critique group, but at press time, the big houses remain unaware of my very existence and I'm now realistic enough to know that a hope for change in that status is as solid as smoke. This is where my geezerhood becomes my new bestie.

I'm a card-carrying, paid-my-dues member of The Most Famous Generation – those ubiquitous, spotlight-loving Baby Boomers. I may never have shouted the radical axiom: Don't Trust Anyone Over 30 but I was there as a contemporary nonetheless. Now, suddenly, here we are facing

Generations X,Y,Z, Millennial, etal. with expected apologies for our very numbers, the purported bane of the financial future of the Social Security System. That factoid is not our fault – don't hate us because we somehow managed to survive to > twice the age of trustability. I'd like to hear what Erma would say about all that. But I digress into social commentary when what I really want to point out is perspective.

Back in my wonder years I would have felt a strong aversion to the humiliation of having my creative writing efforts so soundly ignored by the industry. As I near my golden years, I suffer no longer from such an undeveloped self-image. I still want everyone to like my work, but if someone doesn't . . . it's not like I'll be voted off the island or anything.

Just before hearing the first whispered summons of my muse, purchasing a Thesaurus and plowing into the insanity and unprofitability of the writing world, my life had undergone several personal hardships, as if I had a quota to fill and time was short. I can't know whether I would have felt this need to write if not for those challenges that truly altered my paradigm, my outlook, my expectations. *No Pain, No Gain* has morphed from motivational workout slogan into reassuring validation for the darker chapters of life. I hasten to add, though, that I DO NOT sign up for further heartache merely to gain new writing material.

I can recall, just after I became personally computerized in 1999, all the dire and serious warnings about the drastic changes that could occur simply because on midnight of a single day we would leap from one century to the next. Catastrophic interruptions to life as we knew it were incessantly forecast. But I received no heads-up, felt no tingly spidey-sense about the unexpected health and personal family issues that would cause such aftershocks and unearth an obscured dream.

So, Big House recognition or no, I have found a deeply satisfying outlet for all these ideas or concepts or figments. Whatever their labels, wherever their disposition, I consider their existence to be a reward, a prize. Past that? Well, I'll just have to stay tuned.

If, at the end of my life I'm given the opportunity to lucidly account for my choices, I'd rather smile and say, "Alas, I never became a bestselling author," than the infinitely more regrettable, "Alas, I was too afraid to go for it." I may never catch Erma Bombeck, but if she can see me, I'll bet she's saying, "You go, baby boomer girl!"

# Bobbie McGee and Me

*A brain challenge for this writer.
Watch for camouflaged lyrics.*

We pulled onto Highway 61 at 5:48, twelve minutes early. I always checked the time at this exact spot. I had to dodge a white Nissan whose driver was trying on each lane for size, likely giddy with the freedom of a near-deserted highway at this early hour on a sleep-in Saturday morning. I had no desire to play bumper cars.

Bobbie was already asleep, but roused when I swerved, registering her displeasure at being disturbed from her tortuous nest: a colorless pillow and a ratty throw made from faded blue jeans. How she was consistently able to disappear into sleep within three or four minutes of departure was one of my serious pet jealousies. I couldn't sleep in a moving car if you slipped me Propofol with a tequila chaser. Bobbie said this proved I had no useful imagination. Well, at least I was reliable and showed up at work on time, traits for which she had no affection or value. Predictability was as terminal a condition as Stage Four brain cancer, an opinion she'd actually given ... out loud.

But I was stuck with her, this busted flat, unkempt, scattered, unapologetic slip of a chick wearing a perpetually dirty red bandana. She owned no wheels except her scooter, but was as adept as a travel agent at arranging transportation, complete with layovers and transfers, to her destination du jour. And she had no bias against or fear of hitching when necessary.

We were headed north to Heber Springs; Bobbie would continue west with a connecting ride from yet another acquaintance – one of many that she kept tucked away in several opportune places. This three-hour trip would be only the start of her eighteen-hour excursion but I'd be in the lap of luxury for the next three nights. My new husband was meeting me for a birthday gala: a secluded cabin with a deck over the river. He'd also mentioned a surprise, but this trip was so special that I felt like I deserved no more, nothing beyond the fact that My Love cared enough to conceptualize, plan and orchestrate such a gift.

I had met and married my amazing husband only one year earlier. Joe was not a fan of Bobbie's and made no bones about it. He worried about my responsibility in her life, but I had disclosed the circumstances before we married, and I hadn't yet seen a good way to change things or move them forward. Bobbie was just one of those people – her support system was vital to her survival and this fact was frequently tested and proved. Once, four or five years ago, we were on this same route and she got lost just outside Salinas while we were stopped for gas and snacks at a ginormous truck stop. Our friend Janis says that Bobbie's all about 'playin' soft and feelin' good.'

We all know it's true. Even my husband Joe, who has become more tolerant of Bobbie since his mother became needy due to a hip replacement. He moved in with his folks six weeks earlier and this weekend getaway to the river would be time off for good behavior while his half-sister cared for their mom.

Bobbie snarfed while turning toward the passenger door, face smooshed up against the window as though it was a feather pillow. After about thirty seconds, the fingers on her left hand fluttered as she smiled again. She dreams a lot and claims to recall every one of them.

My cell phone rang. Joe. Yes, I'm still on schedule, Bobbie's ride will be on time – she always is.

Bobbie slept the whole way, waking only when we pulled into the Café Joplin where I could see Cass sitting in a window booth.

Refreshed, Bobbie literally hopped out of the car and swirled around to retrieve her two bags from the back seat. Then she returned to the front and gracefully gathered her bedding in a practiced motion.

We all sat at the table inside, Cass and Bobbie chattering of yesterdays and tomorrows. After ten minutes I discovered I was continuously allowing my mind to daydream of my husband and our weekend plans. I confessed, hugged Cass and Bobbie, brushed crumbs off Bobbie's chin and said good-bye.

Bobbie waved at me through the window, but she was talking animatedly to Cass, multitasking. I tooted the horn and pulled back out to the highway, letting them slip away.

😎☮😎

# Night Noises

*Fictional salute to a favorite Colorado town,
images of which floated through
my brain as I wrote.
This is my favorite of all my stories.*

Sylvia sat on the balcony, tucked out of view just one story above the western section of Azure's two-block downtown. She'd been lounging with her eyes closed until she heard the familiar shuffling sound of Midnight Man as he strolled the street below delivering his nightly discourses to an audience of himself. Intermittently, Sylvia could pick out an actual English language word, but typically the man spoke in a tongue most certainly not from any country or culture on this planet. She checked her watch; yes, he was out early tonight ... which would make him *Eleven-Fifteen* Man. Good one. She'd have to remember to tell Bertie when he came up in a while.

The neighborhood eccentric drifted out of range and Sylvia enjoyed a coveted moment of frosty silence. She sipped raisiny merlot from a coffee cup. No time to do today's dishes, or yesterday's either, so the mug served as a surrogate wine glass. Her bare feet were a stark contrast to the rest of her body which was wrapped in a patchwork throw from the bedroom. The abbreviated quilt had been salvaged from one that her Granny Linwood hand-made a century or two ago. Sylvia had cut out the most resilient portion of the not-so-gently-used quilt and sewed a new border around it. It looked nice; Granny would approve.

The door of Bullwinkle's, the bar just up the street, opened to expel several patrons onto the street. Sylvia sat upright to check the scene as the momentary silence surrendered to the sudden laughter that filled the sharp night air. The departing group of people headed west and made their way to a van parked just past the intersection of Evergreen and Main. Sylvia sat back, anxious for the merrymakers to leave the area; a palpable yearning to revisit the prior calm. The van's engine sounded like a race car, rumbling like earth-thunder. Sylvia startled, sat up again and turned to award the offending vehicle her best schoolmarm frown. The van's departure from the area created a deep contrast that made the subsequent quiet even more so.

This was Sylvia's favorite part of any day. She could take off her shoes and let her weary toes be as one with the starry night. The Rocky Mountain star landscape was unbelievable, even through the muted streetlights of downtown Azure. And she was still astonished, even after living here for six and a half years, by the stars' virtual closeness. Temperate stargazing evenings were so few that she planned her non-working hours around them. Bertie had even bought her a down sleeping bag thingie that she could snuggle in during very early spring and late autumn; she would be utilizing it again very soon. It was now September and she was already jealous of the calendar days remaining before serious winter became again the boss of her treasured nighttime respites.

She thought about the evenings spent out of doors back home in rural Arkansas. Almost a different planet. There, the evenings for comfortable outdoor lounging numbered even fewer. Heat, humidity and/or wretched, blood-sucking insects kept most folks inside. And the night noises – the tree frogs, crickets, cicadas and other concealed but vocal beasties - made it an impossible dream to experience a silent night. Granny Linwood would fan herself and say that the night creatures were merely "crabby from the heat, same as us." When she'd lived down South, Sylvia hadn't enjoyed sitting outside, even in cooler seasons when those regional warm-weather annoyances had closed for the season.

A dog's bark banished the fleeting silence. Sylvia recognized the sound as that of B.T., the Knittols' Boston Terrier. She raised herself to peer over the opaque barrier and call a soft hello to Bruce Knittol who held a dog leash in his outstretched hand. He greeted her in return and muttered something about bladders the size of marbles. Sylvia chuckled, hoping he was referring to B.T. She heard the muscular dog's deep-throated growl once more a few minutes later and then no more.

A car passed below and clunked through a pothole. Another drove by slowly and parked in the space vacated by the drag-racer van. Three car doors slammed and in eight seconds the door to Bullwinkle's opened, late night bar sounds erupting as if someone had turned up the volume of the scene for an instant.

The small terrace where Sylvia sat shuddered briefly; Bertie was on his way up. When the ground floor door was pulled tightly closed it sounded and felt like it was wholly attached to the structure, as if the terrace bone was connected to the door bone. Bertie said those tremors put him in mind of his former hometown, San Francisco. At this time of night, the shudder also prompted a tinge of guilt for Sylvia. She always felt bad on the nights when she hadn't stayed behind to help her husband close down their café – Bert's, or the store, as they called it. But some evenings, Bertie told her to am-scray, get lost, vamoose. He knew what a half hour of solitude at day's end meant to her.

Bertie came outside with a frosty longneck beer and kissed his wife before repositioning a chair so he could sit and put his own feet up, remaining affectionately close to his wife's chair. He reached over and squeezed her sheathed wrist. They did not speak, as they had been together at the store all day and had run through their allotted dialogue.

Bertie sighed a long breath of relaxation and began to softly hum the theme from *Law & Order*. Sylvia listened to the familiar, guttural melody three times through before she nimbly used her right foot as an icy cattle prod on Bertie's hand, the only exposed skin other than his dog-tired face.

"Yow!" he bellowed as he jerked his hand away. The sound reverberated down the block and back to the terrace/haven, bouncing off the Elk Horn Hotel, the tallest building on the street. Sylvia glared at him with only one eye. He was grinning, penitently silent. His rebuked hand was now sheltered in the pocket of his hoodie jacket.

A sudden, frosty gust of wind spilled the mail that Sylvia had brought outside with her. The electric bill ended up on the jute rug, the flyer for an end-of-season sale slapped up against the half-wall of the balcony before sliding down when the gust calmed to a lazy breeze. Bertie shivered and made his lips go "brrrrrrr." Sylvia hurriedly retrieved the papers before re-wrapping the quilt even tighter around her.

The rich red wine warmed her from the inside so she didn't yet feel uncomfortable enough to leave her chilly refuge for the warmth of the bed. Besides, going inside would require a physical exertion that, at that exact moment, seemed as strenuous as jogging in high heels on the bald peak of a 14er. Inhaling a generous helping of the blowy mountain air, Sylvia noticed that the stars were disappearing from the northwest. She became aware of a new, croaky soundtrack to the ethereal scene before her: the snores of an exhausted café owner.

His left hand had fallen from his pocket and hung limply at his side. His equally exhausted wife/business partner smiled at how the hand twitched sporadically; Chef Bert was probably dream-cooking.

Sylvia groaned at the thought of physical effort, but Bertie would freeze if she let him snooze al fresco for very long. The breeze was picking up and his zippered jacket had draped open. Okay, just a couple more minutes, she decreed.

She thought about their careers before moving to the mountains – she an accountant, he an electrical contractor. Steady incomes, good life, but typically monotonous and lacking. They were now living the ultimate cliché: discarding their safe but unfulfilling existence to run away to the Colorado Rockies for the sequel of their time on earth. Living the dream. Happily ever after. Owning and running a business in a seasonal tourist area had proven to be tougher than they could have guessed, but then again, the perks were as awesome as advertised and there were few dull days.

Sylvia's nighttime daydream was rudely interrupted by the one-sided phone conversation she could hear from just beneath her position. A young guy was trying to convince an unheard listener that he'd spotted Will Farrell that very night in Bert's. Sylvia smiled. She and Bert had indeed hosted several celebrities in their snug little mountain eatery, but she had not seen Will Farrell nor anyone else well-known that night. Well, unless you counted Midnight Man.

Sylvia mused that Bertie's snoring had assumed a cadence that somehow comically mimicked the *Law and Order* theme, or maybe she was just that tired herself. She gathered her quilt and the mail, and nudged Bertie somewhat awake. As she watched him wobble in half-sleep toward the terrace door, she glimpsed the evening's first snowflake and paused to enjoy for just a moment the unrivaled, pristine silence of the wafting dime-sized ice crystals.

😎 ☮ 😎

# Alternative Rock

*You may say I'm a dreamer ....*

Buddy stood just outside the Green Room, gathering as much personal presence and gravitas as this gig needed. He was tired, and may even be approaching *sick* and tired, but that hadn't ever made a difference. His fans were gracious enough to support him still, even though he had scaled back personal appearances and given up concerts all together. His music still sold at a level that most any surviving old rocker would be happy with ... even 60-plus years down the road.

On this guest shot for late night TV's Jett Hemingway, Buddy would necessarily be asked to recall some of his rock and roll life, pitch his upcoming memoir, *That'll Be Buddy Holly,* and, of course, revisit that famous plane crash in '59. The familiar lumps formed in his throat and his gut as he recalled the aftermath of that frigid night. His memories take him back only to the next morning; the details of the actual event have never emerged from the black hole.

But he'd learned decades ago that it would be the most asked question about his life and it surely is a significant thing to survive a plane crash, so he always replied graciously to the inevitable and repetitious queries.

As the introductory strains of *Peggy Sue* reached Buddy's ears, he straightened his glasses and moved toward the curtains. Jett met him with an outstretched hand while the audience erupted, fewer high-pitched girl screams than in the glory days, but Buddy picked up one or two, isolated an enthusiastic fan in the audience and blew kisses before taking his seat at the desk.

As he sat, a male voice from the other side of the audience called out, "BudDEEEE!" to which Buddy offered a salute. More applause and a few woots and whistles. It was nice to hear.

Jett took control. "Nice specs there, Buddy. You got, like, dozens of 'em or what?"

"Yeah, I do, gifts from fans mostly. Retro are me. Stuck in a fashion rut, I guess."

"Nah, man, you know it's your trademark. Hey, like, when you want to go incognito, what'd'you … maybe wear rimless … or contacts?" Jett gestured as he drew the picture.

"Well, I can't do contacts so I either just be myself or squint to the point of headaches." Buddy took off his glasses, comically squinted and reached out as though blind.

"Yeah, I read something about the contacts thing … being related to your injuries in the plane crash?"

"Well, yeah, I guess, though I'd never tried to wear them before that. It'd be a shock to do the face plant I did and NOT come away with more changes than just a rebuilt right cheek … well, and the broken ribs, right ankle, yadda yadda."

"It was a miracle, for sure. And your singing was not affected, right?"

"Not my voice, no. The tough part about that was having to say good-bye to my cohorts, my pals, and then think about moving forward, living a life that was denied to the others. You know, survivor's guilt and all that."

"Your tribute album to Bopper and Richie – that was your first step?"

"Yeah, but Maria was behind that ... um, thanks, Babe! After our oldest, David, was born just a few months after the crash, I was finally feeling like singing again, though I was still laid up. I'd written a song or two but she suggested maybe a project to pay tribute, and my mind just grabbed it and ran. I got a little bit crazy ... felt like I didn't even want to eat, drink or breathe until I was singing again, making it happen. All that stuff's in the book." Buddy did a cartoon wink at the audience, camping it up.

"Yeah, you called in the Crickets and the rest, as they say, is rock and roll history," Jett said as Buddy's voice came through the sound system singing just a few bars of *Oh Donna* and fading into *Chantilly Lace*.

Jett commented that the tribute album went platinum, boosted the sales of the original artists' albums as well. After the applause died down, Jett took a commercial break during which he told Buddy that his new book would be the next topic.

Full screen image of the memoir's cover led into the next segment which opened with Buddy signing a copy to present to Jett. Then on a big screen behind them images of Buddy through the years at concerts and with other rock legends began to scroll by.

Jett asked, "So, here we are. You've been singing for a long time. Lived the life. Some would say you've lived two. Make us want to read this book."

"Well, this audience may be willing to read it since they're all getting a copy to take home with them."

The audience rewarded the singer/author with wild enthusiasm before he continued. "And, for those out there who may not care about MY life, there are lots of stories from my touring days. Funny or otherwise interesting bits about lots of stars. Like, of course, the Beatles. And Monterey Pop Festival back in '67 – I was in the audience, then had lunch with Paul Butterfield, and Janis invited herself along. Yeah, mm hmm. I toured with Jimmy Morrison before he quit The Doors to be a preacher. Yup, he's still a cool dude. One story I'll tell you today: Mama Cass Eliot was visiting with my wife Maria in … oh … it was just after Y2K and all that craziness. Anyway, we were talkin' shop and she ended up giving me *If Only,* my first hit of the new millennium. She said she was thinking of sending it to Elton John but since I was the one standing in front of her, she'd let me have it."

Jett said, "Wow. Very generous of her, and definitely Sir Elton's loss. Wonder why she didn't record it herself?"

"That was during a time that she was having some kind of issue with her throat – she didn't announce that at the time – and she wasn't sure she'd get to record again. Of course, we know she got over that, but at the time it was a big question mark."

"I think she's written songs for Katy Perry and Reba McEntire too," Jett commented.

"She's great, AND a great talent. Also, of course you've shown some of the pictures I include in the book and there is a unique feature – I asked several of my buddies to sign the manuscript, like we used to do in our high school yearbooks. There's some funny stuff there – inside each cover … but there's also some of the traditional 'Stay as sweet as you are' kind of stuff, and some great – and I do mean _great_ – doodling or graphics or whatever." Buddy laughed behind his hand. "Be sure to check out John Lennon's. He's always been the funniest Beatle. Yeah yeah yeah."

Jett perked up. "Um, d'you have any inside info about a rumored 6$^{th}$ reunion of the Fab 4?"

"Well … not to spill the beans or anything … nah, seriously. George asked my opinion and I gave it. That's all I know."

The audience raised the volume for a communal groan, "Awwwwwww."

"Of course you were FOR a reunion?" Jett encouraged.

"Yeah, I mean, I'm a fan too. But, ya know, a lot of us are very far removed from those rockin' kids, with fire in their bellies, history and music to make, live hard and die young stuff. Myself? These 84-year-old vocal cords and my banged-up body cannot do what 19-year-old Buddy Holly could do. I think, to some of us old timers, it may come down to whether our fans would be … disappointed to see us perform decades on. Sometimes it's best to just watch the old videos, ya know."

Jett nodded and said, "Well, I can see all that …. but rock stars still rule, and there's always unplugged performances or …"

"Tell you what," Buddy said as though an idea had just come to him. "I don't know if y'all have heard about an upcoming very special birthday celebration for a certain ... or maybe I should say the biggest ever ... rock icon?" The audience broke loose and wouldn't let Buddy finish for several minutes.

Buddy finally held up his hands to still the crowd while images of Elvis Presley's long life in show business filled the big screen behind him and Jett. *Blue Suede Shoes* played in accompaniment. After a last flamboyant display of their love from the crowd Buddy got to finish his thought.

"Yup, Elvis, the king himself, has asked me to perform at Graceland with him when we tape his 85$^{th}$ birthday celebration. Y'all may just get a song outta me then!"

😎 ☮ 😎

# I'll Have the Irony, Please

*Story that popped into my head after noticing a statue-still woman across the way.*

Susannah:
The coffee tasted like tin but at least it was hot. As cold and damp as I felt after getting caught in the rain, I might've willingly consumed liquid asphalt. Damp? "Sopping wet" was the phrase my Southern mama would've used. Or, "You look like a drownded rat." I had to smile at the memories those trite words brought to mind, colloquial coarseness aside.

    I asked for a refill and ordered a grilled cheese sandwich. Might as well play this nostalgia card all the way through. I shivered involuntarily as I noticed my jacket dripping tiny puddles at the base of my chair onto a floor that could have been painted by Jackson Pollock.

The sandwich turned out to be as big a disappointment as the coffee. A traditional, authentic grilled cheese sandwich is composed of two pieces of white bread, good American cheese, and butter. Three ingredients – hard to botch up. This ... unrecognizable assemblage would be better titled *Not Your Granny's Grilled Cheese*. Shredded white cheese, red peppers, garlic and curly endive on a toasted roll du jour.

I only managed about half the sandwich but the second cup of coffee tasted more of coffee and less like its metal container, so I wrapped both hands around the mug and checked out the room.

Two tables away a woman sat with her back to me. She had long dark hair, a single sitting at a two top. I was captivated by her utter stillness. Me, I'm as fidgety as a long-tailed cat in a room full of rocking chairs. Argh, there I go channeling my mother again. I have a self-diagnosed case of Restless Head-to-Toe Syndrome. Even at home, theoretically relaxed and watching television, I practically wear out my spot on the sofa.

I observed this mannequin/diner while pumping my crossed right leg as though drilling for oil. I could surely fault the two mugs of coffee for at least a part of the involuntary calisthenics.

Anyway, the girl was wearing a gauzy shirt that was dry; she'd obviously come in before the deluge. On her feet were suede moccasins that wouldn't have fared well on a wet sidewalk. She finally did make a motion, running her right hand through her hair revealing a couple of features. Her neck wore a tattoo of bright colors, its composition lost quickly to the curtain of her hair as it cascaded back down, and she flashed a distinctive bracelet of leather and silver that covered most of her forearm. The movement plucked at a foggy memory from the nether regions of my mind, but it wouldn't fully reveal itself.

As I watched her settle back into a statue state, I decided she was likely an artist of some kind. The shops in this district were moving away from the former barber shops, drug stores and dress boutiques to favor more bohemian, artsy ventures. That could be why this café shunned prosaic, homely menu items like American cheese on white bread, offering foofy cheese and shrubbery leaves on weird bread. I picked up and perused the menu on my table, something I had neglected to do when I'd had the yen for the sandwich. No pot roast, fried chicken, meatloaf or French fries, and the closest thing to a burger was a Portobello mushroom look-a-like, with or "sans" Provolone cheese. Puh-leez.

With no hint of a letup in the downpour, I ordered a slice of a happy-sounding dessert called Soleil Tart and smiled – I could order some sun on-a-plate if not from the weather department. I spent a few minutes with my datebook and the "tart" that did an uncanny impersonation of good old lemon meringue pie, "sans" the egg white.

The two tall cups of coffee made their presence felt so I sought out the restroom – it was beyond the statue/artist girl. Good. Maybe I could see her face. Why this had become so important to me I couldn't say.

I passed her table and turned to push open the door which was inevitably marked "Femmes" in a flowing, trés self-obsessed script. Glancing back in statue girl's direction, I saw that she had bent to retrieve her bag from the floor near her feet. Still no face, but there came back once more that spark of a memory, still unformed and entirely unsatisfying.



Bobbi Jo:

I looked up to observe the theatrical entrance of the new customer. She was all brief case, frizzed hair and attitude. And ... yikes, someone I didn't care to make eye contact with. As she went through her mad-at-the-world efforts at sitting down, I eased from my seat to the chair opposite. With my back to her I may be spared the possibly of recognition and interaction.

Seeing someone from your past can put you right back there, no matter how recent or distant. It's frequently a pleasant journey, but not today. Susannah was one of the kids at school who caused me to choose separate classes back then and made me avoid class reunions ever since. If Lynn Ann and KayKay show up, I may be forced to leave through the bathroom window. Ha. Wouldn't be the first time.

That trio of girls had been only indirectly hateful to me, but they repeatedly made overt efforts to occupy space that was as far from me as was humanly possible – way over there in the cootie-free zone. The one decent memory I have of them involved a school trip to visit a junior college; was that tenth or eleventh grade? Mercy, what a bus full of giggly, boisterous, dramatic females unleashed from the tedious confines of the classroom. The overpowering aura that resulted from the mingling of what seemed to be every fragrance of perfume, deodorants and hair spray on the planet had been the instigation for that particular pit stop.

Our teacher Miss Stallnon hadn't scheduled a stop for another thirty miles. I sat in my seat, growing queasier with every pothole, thinking that if I attempted to be utterly motionless maybe my insides would remain intact and I would live past that day. I was absolutely <u>not</u> going to barf right there on that bus with the entire known universe watching.

Susannah and Lynn Ann were feeling the nauseations as well and sent an unaffected KayKay to plead with Miss Stallnon to make a mercy stop. The teacher relented and we got our bathroom break shortly. We three green-around-the-gill girls raced to the gas station restroom ahead of the others, but the burst of fresh air must have revived us and we each gratefully avoided the bleak prospect of ending up the subject of a humiliating class legend. As we silently applied moistened paper towels to our faces and touched up our makeup we heard a commotion at the door. Apparently it was stuck, but the girls outside thought we had locked it. We heard dramatic moans and pleas and I went over to try pulling on the handle. It was truly jammed and I had to yell out to them to go get help.

It was decided that the other girls would make do with the men's restroom while we three waited – in awkward discomfort – release from our ceramic-tiled prison. All of us had tried to get the stubborn door to budge, but no. Yadda yadda, we eventually had to turn the trash can upside down and use it as a booster to climb up and out the window to a ladder the store manager had placed outside.

If this had been an episode of a TV sitcom, the three captive girls would have bonded over the graceless but amusing incident and then remained lifelong friends, telling and retelling the story over the years. Each girl would recall her version of the goofy story in a wavy-edged daydream scene, enlarging and embellishing details until it hardly resembled the original reality show script. Tearful, nostalgic laughter would be shared by all. Tra la.
But in the real world, this episode had not been worthy of a TV writer's notice. We three had been pleasant to each other throughout the balance of the trip, half-heartedly joking with all the other girls about being "head-locked." But we organically resumed our social distances when back on home turf. I can honestly say I don't remember making eye contact with any of them for the remainder of high school.

And now here I sit, years later, once again attempting to achieve invisibility in order to avoid a disagreeable occasion.

Hold on … this is unacceptable behavior for an adult who has lived a creative, eventful life. I'm no longer that self-conscious, nerdy kid, desperate but incapable of hacking the secret password to gain entry to the hot crowd up there on teenager Mt. Olympus. This ends now. I'll just get my purse and visit the restroom and then go over and have a mature conversation. …

☻☮☻

# Karaoke Summer

*Some of these events happened, some did not.*

    I was brand-newly separated from a 33-year marriage -- the only life I had known after my childhood. I often joked that I moved from my parents' home straight into my husband's. Like everyone, I learned that my life would eventually change yet again as I aged, but what I had most certainly *not* foreseen was a time in late middle age when I would be single, unmarried, alone; sing along with Tammy – d-i-v-o-r-c-e-d. As sheltered and encased as I had always been, the way I chose to live those first few months of the rest of my life came from somewhere out in my own personal left field.

An acquaintance of my aunt owned a shabby little resort near a lake in North Central Texas. Popular as an annual vacation and reunion destination for dozens of families, its glory days were decades in the past. I allowed my aunt to set up a situation for me there based on fundamental needs: for distance from my failures, for the opportunity to have new adventures and build new memories, and as trite as it sounds, to begin again. The reactions of my family to my new job were predictable: surprised (You're moving where?), relieved (You found a job!?), and worried (All by yourself??). My aunt expressed the consensus: "We figured *your* marriage would last until death."

Well. Not so much.

I left for the job only three weeks after the actual separation had occurred. I was chomping at the bit with a tangible yearning to shed the heavy yoke of carrying, for so long, my marital skeletons. Even that first summer, I felt no loneliness, fear, regret or depression. I had dealt with all that unpleasantness during the last year my husband and I remained legally yoked, pre-emptive strikes to block any future visitations of all those bitter, disruptive Coulda Shoulda Wouldas. I was sure I was doing the right thing, and in that mode I tossed my hat into the future ala Mary Tyler Moore.

I moved a few belongings into one of the guest rooms that the motel reserved for seasonal staff. Since I was only three hours' drive from my hometown, I could make occasional trips home to retrieve any of my stored stuff. In choosing this particular situation, my thinking had been to stay near enough to my family that they could come to grasp that I was not some wild, hormonal, repressed middle-aged cliché off on a quest to "find myself." But while I earnestly hoped my loved ones would trust that I had only responded to an incurable problem in the best way I could, it was enough for me that <u>I knew</u>. I needed this geographical gap for many, many reasons, some of which I wouldn't discover until long past that summer I ran away from home.

Most of the rest of the small staff of the motel were townies. Ann, Georgia and Butchy were local, Lee was the owner/manager. My fellow quasi-transients were Junior, a perennial maintenance man/king of the road, and Laney, another single lady with rambling shoes with whom I would share duties and trade days off.

I came to know each of these diverse personalities over the course of only five months. I learned that fifty-ish Butchy had a harem of girlfriends and drove a rusty, anonymous old car with a swiss-cheesed muffler. He ranked about an

8.5 on my creep-o-meter so I gave him wide berth. Junior and I maintained a strictly nine-to-five relationship. Ann and Georgia were two cheery longtime pals who had worked together at three different resorts and were counting the days until retirement (two more years) when they and their husbands planned to travel. Lee may have been the owner of the property and the business, but he owned little in the way of a personality. Dry as dust.

Lee and his wife Alice had lived next door to my aunt's family for twenty-something years before buying The Lakeside Inn – which would have been more correctly named something less charming, like *The Motel Out Toward the Lake*. Junior pulled his multi-patched, rickety camper to each of his recurring gigs. Laney had traveled from Florida where several months previous she had left her handsome but shiftless husband sitting on a dock in a bay. Naturally, I saw in Laney a serendipitous comrade.

My protected, "ordinary" existence was so unlike Laney's that we could have represented two different species. It wasn't that she was sophisticated or cultured, but she'd seen so much and had lived so radically differently from me. I was fascinated that our friendship was so immediate, so effortlessly organic. It could be, too, that twisting her ankle the day before I arrived helped to cement a beginning.

I drove the two of us to Wal-Mart on the second evening of my new life. After familiarizing myself with my sparse quarters, I needed accouterments and Laney was merely bored from the effort of remaining therapeutically prone for two days. We joked that she could ride in the kiddie seat of my grocery cart before choosing instead a more sensible alternative – the cumbersome motorized buggy for disabled shoppers.

Our mutual nicknames were chiseled in place that evening in Wal-Mart. Laney proved to be a clumsy cart driver, comically bouncing the rig off several end-cap units. Once when she gingerly stepped off the cart to examine a display of brightly colored cargo bags, she somehow ended up in a heap on the floor surrounded by red, blue and yellow canvas. Unscathed, she threw her hands up and laughed – a typical response to her frequent foibles, as I was to learn. I helped her back into the buggy and attempted to right the display of bags but they kept cascading back down onto the floor. We were helpless with hilarity. A twenty-first century Lucy and Ethel were born – sans Lucy's carrot-red hair and Ethel's frumpy house dresses.

When we had laboriously navigated through the checkout area, I told my brand new pal that I could see how she had twisted her ankle while performing the basic task of stepping off the curb just outside her motel room. She proceeded to count on her fingers a veritable litany of prior injuries, the only serious ones a badly bruised thigh and a compound fracture of the cheek bone that had left a scar. Both had resulted from up-close-and-personal contacts with over-zealous pets.

Thus accustomed to working while injured, Laney's twisted ankle did not prevent her from training me for my new duties. Our season would start a scant ten days after I reported for work, so there was overtime to be had right out of the gate. I fell into bed on those nights, sleeping better than I thought possible. *Cathartic* is too small a word to describe how wonderful it was that my biggest problem during that time was loading the cart with enough supplies to perform my low-tech housekeeping job.

Typically, the motel was either filled with large, boisterous families or sparsely occupied with the garden variety summer visitor. One day, a weary traveler came in just after lunch and I helped her register. Mrs. Gillette was not the enthusiastic, chipper guest we usually dealt with but she did leave me with something to smile about. As she plodded toward the door with her room key and paperwork I offered the obligatory, "Have a nice day!" to which she quipped, "Yeah, well, some days just refuse to be nice, don't they?" I've never again heard that overworked, artificially-sincere expression without recalling her cheerless rebuttal.

Laney and I became what I can best describe as brand new old friends. We frequently went shopping, tried out various restaurants or relaxed outside in the evenings discussing our lives, our futures, our dreams. Giggling like adolescents was what we did most often. Possibly, we were both in desperate need of comic relief from our recent, somewhat similar difficulties. There were numerous Lucy/Ethel moments: one day at work Laney turned over the loaded housekeeper's cart, spilling toilet paper, soaps, sheets and towels all over the sloping sidewalk. We both had to sit down on the sidewalk, giving over to rabid laughing spasms before we tidied up the calamity – immediately after the boss walked by. Lee had frowned at us, shook his head and walked on. Later he commented to Laney that he now understood why I called her *Lucy*. Lee made a joke – alert the media.

One pastime that Laney and I didn't share was karaoke. Laney was a frustrated country and western warbler. Jed Heaslett, the owner of one of Laney's favorite downtown haunts, told her that the only thing standing in the way of her stardom was her utter lack of talent – an opinion which deterred her not one bit.

On the occasion of her fifty-fifth (double nickels) birthday in early July, Laney begged me to go with her to Jed's Shed for a celebration. Ann, Georgia and Butchy were coming, she whined. I gave in, mostly because I personally believe that birthdays are a pretty big deal. If it would make my new pal happy for me to just show up, I'd be there.

Nothing prepared me for the atypical evening that I would have.

The birthday girl costumed herself in a blingy little number that had Jed referring to her as The Rhinestone Cowgirl – uninspired stage name, maybe, but strictly accurate. The outfit boasted spangles, beads, sequins and, yes, rhinestones. The trim circling her western hat threatened to blind the crowd as the spotlights mirrored from it like an out-of-orbit disco ball. Her black blouse sported a glittery cursive "L" at her left shoulder, shades of Laverne DeFazio. The pink thrift store cowboy boots had been painstakingly festooned with Christmas tree tinsel and jingle bells - in July. The outfit was louder than the singer.

I sipped my Dr. Pepper and smiled long and hard at Laney's show-biz getup, as well as the persona that it fashioned. She sang a tinny *Satisfaction* that would have appalled the Rolling

Stones, and closed her act with an ear-wrenching Loretta Lynn song, *Coalminer's Daughter*. I felt grateful that she hadn't chucked it all and moved to Nashville with stars in her eyes. No way – not gonna happen. But her moves weren't bad at all. Her physical grace far exceeded her vocal efforts, and I marveled at how this was the same woman I was continually pulling up from a floor or off some obstacle during her less graceful hours at the day job.

After her songs, Laney was the belle of the bar. She flitted among her fans, visiting her co-workers' table only intermittently. It was fun to watch her enjoy herself so much.

Co-worker Butchy had backed out of coming and Ann and Georgia had, like me, come only to support Laney. More than once I caught them glancing at their watches. They'd probably prearranged an acceptable time to leave and were politely sticking it out. We talked mostly about work, telling funny or interesting guest stories we couldn't mention while on duty. Bar owner Jed played disk jockey or karaoke jockey or whatever, and between songs cajoled Laney's friends to "come on up and sing." We shook our heads and waved our hands in a firm negative, but just before ten o'clock – Ann and Georgia's apparent curfew – the three of us gave in and went onstage, agreeing only to sing one verse of *Happy Birthday* in honor of Laney.

I wish I could tell you how the next event occurred, but I guess I've blacked that part out. Maybe somebody slipped something into my virginal Dr. Pepper. Maybe the body snatchers invaded. All I remember for sure, even six years later, is the unexpected sound of *me* singing a solo to a whooping, clapping audience. *I Will Survive*, in my best Gloria Gaynor. About halfway through the song, Laney popped up onstage, moving directly in front of the stage lights. She twirled around with her hatband reflecting a zig-zaggy spectrum of colored lights and suddenly, Jed's Shed is an 80's disco! I sang the last note before dissolving into self-conscious giggles. I promise, it felt like someone else was performing – that the crowd applauded a talented but invisible star who stood behind me.

Ann and Georgia had been standing alongside their chairs during the catchy, thumpy tune performing a comically stiff rendition of the old disco dance, The Bump. As I breathlessly approached our table, they high-fived me and made whoop whoop noises – a sight and sound that set off communal hilarity. They were formless dancers and unwieldy whoopers, but they were totally in the moment.

Laney had not ceased bowing and pirouetting onstage. I sat in my chair to catch my breath and watch her eyes sparkle, whether from the spotlight itself or the joy of being therein, I couldn't tell.

The small crowd began clapping in unison, chanting for me to encore. After an initial, firm dismissal of that crazy notion, the spirit of the evening flourished and finally prevailed. I stepped back up on stage, shy again. What would I sing? Laney and I had a quick conference and then the opening notes of *Girls Just Wanna Have Fun* swelled up and possessed us. It was nuts.

Somehow I was persuaded to solo *Judy's Turn to Cry*, topped off with a finale of *Love Potion Number Nine*. People were flinging praise and cheers in my direction like they meant it. Laney said they were giving me "luv."

I flashed Laney an inquisitive glance to see how this bizarre scenario was affecting her. Would she be resentful of my enthusiastic reception; did she read this as an affront to her show business dream? That would make me very unhappy.

But no. Laney preened, my biggest fan, hugging me and pumping her fists in the air. "Ethel? You got some splainin' to do!" she yelled Ricky Ricardo-esque into my right ear.

"Long ago and far away," I matched her volume. "Maybe I'll tell you sometime."

Ann and Georgia hugged me and pointed at their watches. I bowed humbly and dismissed my coworkers. Five minutes later my energy stores hit the basement. Laney had to virtually fold me up to take me home. The car ride was blessedly silent as I allowed my heartbeat to calm and my aching throat and chest to recover. I'd made gluttonous demands on my vocal apparatus, and my body was delivering a righteous chewing-out.

Laney and Ann had the next day off, Georgia was housekeeper and I was on the front desk. Of course the only topic of conversation among us that wasn't resort-related was my unlikely debut on the karaoke stage. We laughed and made goofy plans for a "Geezer Karaoke Extravaganza Tour." We told stories of reactions from audience members: the lady with the beehive hairdo who closed her eyes and swayed to the music, the man with his left leg in a cast who enthusiastically chair-danced nonetheless, the group at a table near the restroom who waved the flashlight app on their cell phones. I graciously accepted my friend's praise and participated fully in the light mood that was carrying the day. Until Ann called.

Her husband's younger sister, Trudy, had died very early that morning. Younger than Larry by nine years, Trudy had not been ill, or at least not to the family's knowledge. She'd been a "holy terror" while growing up and had settled only marginally as an adult. She was the kind of lady who wore hats, even here in the twenty-first century. Her style of dress was always "unique," a mélange of colors and patterns that seemed stylish to her, if not to all the other "fashion-challenged, repressed people whose taste is all in their mouths."

Ann unleashed this volume of biography during that brief phone call, either her version of coping or she herself was somewhat in shock. She finally drew a ragged breath and asked me to let everyone know and to have Georgia give her a call later that morning. She and Larry would be at the funeral home that afternoon, along with Larry's only surviving sibling – Arnelda. We spoke for a few more minutes and then I set about informing the others.

Fifty-nine-year-old Trudy Baselton's funeral would be on Thursday. Georgia, her husband Gene, Laney and I decided to go to the visitation at the funeral home, the night before the service.

The insufficient viewing room held a lively sampling of humanity. The mood felt more that of a wedding reception or family reunion than a somber rite of reverent commemoration. Ann met us at the door and hugged each of us. Then she warned, "Now, don't be surprised that Trudy's attire is a bit . . . non-traditional. She left precise instructions, and after Larry and Arnelda got done arguing about it, Larry won and his free-spirited baby sister got her way, one last time, bless her heart."

"Non-traditional" turned out to be a non-accurate description of the way the deceased was presented for her going-away party. She wore one of her hats, a relatively simple, freeform blue canvas style with red trim. But past that, her attire framed a story to tell and re-tell. No sober dress or starchy blouse in which to enter eternity, but a white t-shirt with iron-on letters that spelled out "Thanks for Coming! Loved Ya!" in the center of a tie-died heart shape. Suffice to say that there was *no* way to hold onto our carefully applied, solemn, traditional demeanors. Trudy's proved to be the most fun wake I'd ever attended.

Over the course of the next week, Ann relayed the family's discovery that Trudy had indeed been ill, but for only a few months. Stage Four breast cancer had set up camp in several organs and at diagnosis she decided that there was no reason to put her failing body through the rigors of surgery or treatment that had a zero percent chance of measurable effect. Trudy had not shared the prognosis with any of the family, but they had noted that she had slowed her pace. She had explained a twenty pound weight loss as an effort to attract a younger man – "They like us skinny, ya know." Concerning her sister-in-law's burial garments, Ann could hardly tell the tangled story between tearful guffaws. Arnelda had been mortified by the idea of putting her departed sister's body on display in that "clown suit." It didn't matter to her that this was Trudy's wish—it most certainly was *not* longsuffering Arnelda's wish to be humiliated one last time by her "flaky" sister. Big brother Larry had gently but firmly insisted that Trudy should have whatever she wanted, flaky or not, and the verbal battle commenced. The funeral director finally intervened, politely restated Larry's argument and offered to show Arnelda the paperwork that Trudy herself had completed and signed, a mere seven weeks previous. Arnelda had crossed her arms over a dramatically heaving bosom and tap-tapped a size ten high-heel but issued no further edicts, so the matter was finally concluded. Larry told Ann that he could swear he saw fury, in the form of smoke, escaping his sister's ears from beneath her trendy platinum blond hairdo.

So Ann moved past her loss and things returned to relative sameness for awhile, at least at the motel. Laney and I signed on to be the Tuesday night entertainment at Jed's Shed – a three-week trial run at a regular gig until season's end. The first night we returned to the stage I panicked and sweat bullets – more like cannonballs – reactions that had been absent that first time when everything had been so madly spontaneous. Laney said, "Girl, get over yourself. All you're gonna do is sing and you know how to do that. It ain't rocket science. And I'm right here next to ya. Don't <u>make</u> me get all up in your Kool-Aid, Ethel."

Her earthy diva act worked to put me at ease and I successfully banished my butterflies. As *Lucy and Ethel Sing Karaoke!* we had a great time and, astonishingly, performed weekly to a packed house at Jed's for the rest of the season, after which I retired the microphone and returned home.

This fabulous, challenging, curative, benchmark summer did not segue into sudden stardom or a huge leap into showbiz for either of the karaoke singers. A few months later, "Lucy" met her "Ricky" and retired from "racing the rats" to a small South Carolina community. We still get together occasionally and yes, she's still blinging and singing.

I'm told that Ann, Georgia and their husbands are burning up the highways and runways in retirement travel bliss. Lee and his wife still own the motel – I've been back once as a guest.

Butchy and Junior were merely cameo appearances in my history. Jed's Shed is still a local dive but I understand that Jed sold out and moved to the beach in rural Florida. I think of him when I hear Jimmy Buffet singing *Margaritaville*.

I'm living a quiet, normal life now – or as quiet and normal as is possible in this dynamic new millennium. But my days are so much more rounded, meaningful and satisfying, in part as a result of the summer I stepped – and sang – outside the box.

Thank you, thank you very much! Lucy and Ethel have left the building ….

😎☮😎

# Memory for Sale

*No backstory here. Just an exercise in making stuff up.*

**Billie Jean** surfed radio channels as she drove down the street, so she very nearly missed the sign. But her eyes turned by rote as she passed the house when the *For Sale* sign just clipped her peripheral vision. Her mind shifted into overdrive as she checked the time on the car radio display. Should she turn around and drive by again? Her inflexible morning commute left a ten-minute pad on her arrival time at work. But this was big—big enough to rearrange her precisely-ordered universe, even on her first day back to work after a week's vacation. She would turn around in the Anderson's driveway, or what had once been the Anderson's driveway, and take another look.

On this approach she slowed to a stop at the curb directly in front of what had been her childhood home. The *For Sale* sign was not the only indication that the property was newly on the market. The yard looked better than she'd seen it in several years, and the front door virtually demanded a buyer's attention with its new coat of glossy red paint. This homeowner had obviously been tuning in to those how-to-sell-your-home HGTV shows and had followed the trustworthy advice to the letter. They had even removed the shabby (not in a *chic* way) arbor trellis that someone had put up some fifteen years previous in an apparent attempt to cottage-up the looks of the plain, boxy brick structure.

There were several new plants in an abbreviated flower bed, not exactly haute botanical design, but it rang true that every little bit helped. Billie checked her rear-view mirror and inched her car backwards so she could see the west window – her former bedroom. No change there, same mini blinds, same black paint smudge on the red brick wall just below.

The radio DJ announced the current time, causing Billie to jerk herself back to present-day Monday morning, exiting the 38-year-old memory of how that paint smudge came to be.

Quickly jotting down the name of the real estate company from the sign, she eased back out into the street. Her cell phone rang minutes later as she sat at the traffic light just outside the parking lot of her office building. Recognizing the caller's number she answered the phone, skipped the greeting and said with a smile in her voice, "I'm just outside, you can call off the dogs." She was less than five minutes tardy and her co-worker Annalynn had already decided the worst.

**By lunchtime** Billie's pumped-up imagination had taken her through the make-believe process of buying her childhood home. She had walked through with the real estate agent and asked the proper questions. She'd shaken hands with Carl down at her bank and had a productive interview with him about her mortgage loan. (He had offered her a low mortgage interest rate because they were so happy to have her as a customer.) She'd signed forms in duplicate and triplicate. She had given notice to her landlord and Mr. Jarvis had begged her to stay, claiming she was his best tenant *ever*.

Annalynn stuck her head in Billie's office with her daily call to lunch. Distracted, Billie replied that she was going to stay in today; she needed to do some computer stuff.

Annalynn gawped, went and placed a hand on her friend's forehead to check for fever as she said, "Okay, who are you and what have you done with my friend Billie who goes to lunch with me five days a week, not to mention the occasional Saturday?"

"Sorry," Billie answered. "I'm working on a T.N.T. project."

"Alton's got you working through lunch?" Annalynn asked as she opened her pink plaid insulated lunch carrier and peered inside.

"No, this particular Today-Not-Tomorrow project is for moi. I'll catch you later."

**The lunch** hour seemed more like a lunch minute. Billie ate three bites of a tuna sandwich that she then abandoned as she went online to glean as much information as she could about the house. The *Your New House* website didn't offer a virtual tour of the property at 1968 Memory Lane, only a photo of each room. She was surprised to see that the interior looked remarkably the same as it had when her parents had sold it decades earlier. She couldn't see the carpeting very well, but the yucky pink ceramic tile in the bathrooms looked unchanged and the kitchen cabinets were stained the same tobacco-color. The photo of the back yard was unrecognizable due to a large shed that had been built where her peppermint-striped swing set had been. A dog house sat adjacent and its occupant, a beagle, lounged on the ground in the miniature house's opening. How cozy – very domestic touch.

The selling price was several thousand more than the amount her folks had gotten, but of course one must allow for decades of inflated property values. Perennial renter Billie had never been a property owner so she couldn't guess how the mortgage payment would fit in with her income and present expenses. But she had a phone number for the real estate agent, who, she was sure, could answer all those questions and more.

An appointment was made for that evening to view the house. She was number three on the list, according to listing agent Francie Howard. This news set off a sudden panic alarm in Billie's head; what if someone else made an offer before she could even take a tour?

When she arrived at 6:30 – a full fifteen minutes early, and this after having cruised the place twice, she parked at the curb where she had paused that morning. She had made a quick trip back to her duplex apartment after work to change clothes and check her online auction bid. She had won the coveted antique refrigerator! Yessssss! She confidently deemed this to be a good omen about her chances at buying the house. The fridge was identical to one that her granny had owned – characteristic rounded, matte white exterior with an unexpected turquoise-painted interior. The listing claimed that it "runs great," but who knew, and anyway, she'd find a use for it, whether as refrigerator or objet d'art. It would look perfect in her new/old house.

Francie Howard pulled up momentarily and exited her SUV, dressed for success in chic capris and a tailored jacket, dangly earrings and clinky bracelets up to here. The agent carried a very feminine brief case in a trendy graphic print and greeted Billie by introducing herself assertively. Billie skimmed over her name and the please-to-meetcha part. Her first question was about whether she still had a shot at the house. *Bad, bad negotiator,* she lectured herself. *While you're at it, why don't you just be a total schmuck and offer a thousand more than the list price?*

"Well, I've shown it a few times already but no offers yet. It's a great neighborhood." said Francie. "Shall we go inside?"

They made a leisurely canvass of the interior, followed by a stroll around the backyard where Francie's cell phone rang. Billie made hand gestures that she wanted to go back inside and Francie waved her approval. Billie walked back in the kitchen door and into the living room. She sighed deeply and stood gazing out the front picture window, a million sentiments surfacing in a mental slide show.

Across the street, an old station wagon pulled into the driveway of the house where her childhood friend Sandra Faye Strandlund had lived. Come to think of it, Sandra's mother Euna Raye had driven an identical or similar woodie station wagon circa 1968. How weird was that? Billie blinked her eyes, rubbing the workday's over-pixeled exposure from them. A headache introduced itself.

The two front doors of the station wagon opened and Billie gasped. A woman and a girl who could have been beamed up from the late 1960s exited the vehicle, each carrying what looked to be brown paper bags of groceries. Euna Raye, or the woman who played her, wore a black and white striped dress straight out of a Mary Quant magazine ad. And there came Sandra Faye, wearing bell-bottomed jeans with flower power appliqués around the hems. Billie frowned and told herself she'd made a huge mistake scrimping on both lunch and dinner.

Francie returned to the living room with her phone up to her ear. She looked at her client with an expression of apology both on her face and in her left arm which was raised in a gesture of helplessness. Billie shook her head in forgiveness and motioned for the agent to continue on, hoping that the woman would go back outside. She did.

Billie hastily returned to the big front window to find the very same surreal view. The station wagon remained outside the Strandlunds' house, and now here came a boy down the sidewalk on a blue Schwinn bicycle, a boy she also knew, or *had* known decades previous. Victor T. Pryzborski. Meanest kid in a six-block radius. He had dismembered her Barbie doll during the summer before fourth grade, stole the body parts and later claimed to have cremated the remains. When Billie asked her mom what "cremated" meant, she cried in mourning.

Billie shook herself, and then raised her hand to her forehead. *Please, no*, she thought as she walked back to her old bedroom. She went over to the window that she'd viewed from the street that morning and raised the mini blinds. From this view, everything appeared as it should. She could see the back edge of the new storage shed, so at least the back yard still safely existed in present-day 2008. She closed one eye – why, she couldn't say – and peered out toward the street. Once again, no time warp was in evidence from here; she could see her 2006 model Chevy. *Whew! Still here,* she thought. *I'll go for a big dinner when I'm done, nourish my feeble brain and empty tummy.*

As she left the room she could hear that Francie was still on the phone just outside the back door so she walked furtively to what had been her parents' bedroom. From the window in this room it was hard to see any variation in time. She sprinted back to the living room to steal another hopeful glance outside before the agent returned. On this examination of the Twilight Zone-ish scene that remained unchanged, she noted that the For Sale sign was nowhere in evidence.

Francie finally returned, profusely apologetic about the interruption. Billie said without turning from the window, "Haven't seen one of those in years, huh?" She pointed, hoping not to appear deranged, at the station wagon across the street.

"Really? My sister's family owns one," Francie responded hesitantly.

Billie turned toward the lady and drew in a stunned breath. Francie wasn't Francie anymore, or rather, the face was the same but now she wore a pink tweed jacket and pencil skirt. On her restyled, sprayed-stiff, flip hairdo sat a pill box hat. Billie had a completely irrational thought: "Well, she's no Jackie Kennedy," at the exact moment she felt herself slipping to the floor in a dead faint.

**The first thing** Billie noticed when she woke was that she was lying in the grass. Cobwebs and hazy, ethereal clouds populated her mind and she couldn't think why she'd be in this position. Chiggers and bugs live in the grass, it was certainly no place for people to lounge about. If her mother had said those words once, she'd said them a thousand times.

Suddenly, there was her mother, leaning over her, calling her name and gently patting her face. Billie felt amused at the way her mother showed such concern for her injured daughter one minute and then whipped around to scold her brother Andy, who Billie couldn't see. Now it was coming back to her.

Her mother shouted for Andy to go inside and get a wet cloth and a glass of water. Billie attempted to say something but her mouth wouldn't quite work, so she revisited the attempt to put together how she had come to be in the grass.

She'd been in the side yard … painting a sign? Oh, right, a campaign sign for the class president election. Her best friend Annalynn was a candidate and Billie was painting a stenciled sign on poster board: "Vote for Annalynn! She's Groovy!" Andy had been out back shooting hoops just before he'd come around to the side yard to torment her. Putting her flashes of memory together with the accusations her mother was hurling at Andy, she dimly recalled that he had bounced the ball off the brick wall a couple of times. Then the ball had come in her direction.

Still flat on the ground, she turned her head toward the house where she saw a new round, glossy black spot just beneath her bedroom window. The simple motion caused a shooting pain in her head that brought tears to her eyes and high-pitched alarm to her mother's voice. The haze in her head and the air around her began to darken and she heard Andy explaining that the ball had accidentally hit Billie's saucer of black paint, which "made her freak out and she zigged when she should have zagged," causing her to trip on her poster board project to fall hard against the brick wall.

Billie wanted to report that her brother was too conveniently denying personal responsibility, his usual tactic, that the little creep had thrown the ball directly at her. This time, a noise came out when she tried to speak, but it didn't sound like words. Her anxious mother instructed Andy to go inside and call his father at work.

**Billie knew** nothing else until she rose in slow motion through that bothersome fog yet again. This time she was in a hospital, but she must've been totally out of it while they brought her here. The air smelled of antiseptic which made her tummy roll a bit, and there were beeping sounds coming from somewhere just out of sight. Her family was in the room, but no one was looking at her. As before, her attempts to speak were unsuccessful, but now it was worse – she couldn't seem to move. Not her mouth, not even her fingers.

Young Andy walked slowly to her bed. He looked at her through a gloomy face; in fact, he had a tear track running from his right eye to his chin. He moved his lips, in what might have been a prayer, and then touched his sister's hand gingerly and spoke audibly but softly, "Billie, I am <u>so</u> sorry. You got to wake up. You just GOT to wake up."

*I <u>am</u> awake, numbskull. And git-cher grubby mitts off me. Haven't you done enough?* Billie was horrified that these words in her head didn't make the customary trip through her mouth to the outside world. She concentrated really hard for several minutes but succeeded only in producing an intense fatigue. She'd never been so tired in all her life. Maybe she'd take another little nap ….

**The clouds** of unconsciousness once again divided and cleared, but it seemed to take weeks. Billie saw a blurry image moving about and a voice came to her ears as if someone was turning up the volume. She felt a cold wet cloth on her forehead and her chest was a bit sore, but she was breathing. After taking a minute to semi-collect herself, she tested her voice, "Um, hello?"

"Oh, thank goodness!" the realtor responded, exhaling in relief. She set down her cell phone and dropped to the living room floor beside Billie. "Are you okay?"

"I am SO sorry," Billie responded weakly. "Yes, I'm fine, or ... or... I <u>will</u> be. I just need a minute." Another few minutes and she'd be able to explain. She asked the real estate agent to bring her a glass of water and hoped Francie would take comfort in Billie's responsiveness and lack of panic. It had been a long time since the last episode.

**Thirty-five** minutes later, after the paramedics were sent on their way, Billie apologized again to Francie, the innocent bystander who had hastily performed a rather intense and unnecessary CPR. "Old childhood injury," Billie explained. "I was told to expect random episodes, but they've become very rare. I had even begun to think they were behind me."

Billie rested on the couch in the living room after Francie had taken yet another call and returned to the back yard with Billie's consent. Billie tried to determine the trigger for this flashback. It had literally been years since the last one at the wedding reception of a school friend. Sipping her ice water, she allowed a bit of trepidation to creep in. Could this be related to being back in her childhood home, the site of the original injury? Would it be foolhardy, wistful optimism to think of buying this house? If living here, connecting again to her youth, meant more frequent time-traveling "episodes," well then, no thanks – too much baggage for a major financial decision made during a fit of foolish nostalgia. It is difficult enough to live in the present without impromptu virtual trips back to the sixties. Now, if she could go back in time and *prevent* the brain injury, well then, that would be something else altogether.

The physical effects and implications of the episodes were bad enough, but she had never shared her secret concerns of the worst-case scenario. Would there come an episode where she may not be released from her Distant Past: The Sequel ... doomed to repeat her life, or worse: to relive the painful experience ad infinitum? At her most cognizant she realized that those thoughts sounded more like the plot of a science fiction movie than real life, but today her fears became steeped in credibility when Francie "Jackie Kennedy" Howard entered the living room yet again.

**The next day,** for the first time in years, Billie changed the route she drove to work, freshly apprehensive of being anywhere on Memory Lane, ever.

😎 ☮ 😎

# MONTEREY PAPA

*Fictional story and characters,
inspired after watching video of the
1967 Monterey Pop Festival.*

*This story was published in the anthology:
Stories through the Years, Baby Boomers 2018*


Hildy adjusted her monitor so she could see it from a slouched position in the desk chair. She would have aching neck muscles again tonight but her assignment would run on the evening news and couldn't be done leisurely. She sipped her iced coffee and hit the play button on the third disc of *The Complete Monterey Pop Festival*.

Hooch Conrad had died the night before and Hildy's task was to put together the few pieces of his professional life on film for the requisite homage. Even though Hooch had only had one - no, two Top 40 hits way back in the late sixties. Though he'd be best remembered for eccentric mug shots, one where he'd held up two fingers in a droopy, druggy peace sign. Though he hadn't been on the public scene for thirty years, he'd still get a tribute. The Baby Boomers from her parents' generation in the TV audience ate that stuff up and asked for seconds.

At that groundbreaking concert in Monterey, California circa 1967, Hooch attained notoriety partially because he left the stage without finishing his Number One Hit from that year, *Radio Peace*. To the audience it appeared that he thought he was done when he took an abrupt bow, mid chorus, and left the stage. His ironically titled second release, *Not Enough,* never climbed higher than number twelve on the charts. Denied the important sophomore hit, he faded away into that obscurity reserved for those who had glittered only briefly in the fickle spotlight. He'd pop back up every few years with a misdemeanor or felony, do his time, and slip back into whatever.

*Whatever* apparently caught up with the sad old rocker the night before. His nephew found him unconscious and the EMT's had not been able to revive him. No exotic or legendary exit for Hooch, it was apparently a massive stroke. He'd be cremated later that day and it was buzzed through social media that his ashes were to be auctioned off online. Creepy.

Hildy hadn't yet been born when California's Monterey Pop Festival was staged so she was unfamiliar with the concert, even if she did know a lot about many of its stars. She and her friends were big fans of the Grateful Dead, the Who, and Janis Joplin, both in and out of Big Brother and the Holding Company. Hildy had assumed she'd get a kick out of the concert footage of those favorites, but had been surprised at how much she was getting into the entire production. Maybe she was becoming a connoisseur of music. She even liked some of the Blues. She might play The Paul Butterfield Blues Band for her friends. Could be there was something significant about this golden assembly of rockers from the pivotal era leading up to Woodstock. Millions of Baby Boomers may not be wrong.

It was easy to see from the concert tape that the audience certainly believed something awesome was taking place. Candidly caught on film while history occurred on stage, some spectators were in worlds of their own making, some swayed, some rocked hard. Hildy was captivated by the hairstyles, the makeup, the sunglasses, the fashions, how relatively organic these young people appeared – caught on film in unstaged leisure. They seemed soft and genuine – less slick, hard and cynical than the look in the eyes of today's kids. A dichotomous reaction when one recalled that the Boomers' generation became famous for its mass mutiny against status quo.

Hildy wondered what was going on in the thoughts of these kids as they sat en masse on the cusp of societal change. The world was a vastly different place in 1967 from the perspective of 2018, but also dissimilar from most. Who could've known the future of rock and roll? Who could've guessed the outcome of the burgeoning anti-war, civil-rights, women-are-people-too awareness from the turbulent, hyper-aware mid-century? Hildy decided to follow up on these questions by talking with her mother – if not a radical participant then certainly an eye-witness.

The Mamas and the Papas were treating her to their distinctively sweet harmony when her eyes flashed her brain a morsel of recognition from a shot of the audience. The camera focused on a girl who had been in several previous shots, probably because she was very cute - long straight, bangless hair, her left cheek painted with the words PS I LUV YOU. A continuous smile on her face, she lip-synced the lyrics and was obviously very tuned in to the concert vibe. But Hildy didn't know this girl from the man in the moon; she was more interested in a guy behind and to the smiling girl's right.

She hit the short reverse and sent Mama Cass back a verse. Then she sat up straight to better view the impending crowd scene. There! She froze the picture and inched it back, back, back until just before the man came into three-quarter view. Then she played the five second scene at several speeds. The LUV girl partially blocked him, but Hildy was very nearly convinced that she was looking at a video image of her father from 1967!

**Two hours** later, the newsroom editor straightened her impossibly curled body to stand on her feet; the right leg was pins-and-needles numb. If Hildy didn't take a break she was afraid the image of the corrugated awnings from the mid-century Monterey fairgrounds might be permanently burned into her subconscious. She'd torn herself away from this greedy new quest for more shots of her late father to finish the film clip on Howard "Hooch" Conrad. The scene of his premature exit from the concert stage was added to the ubiquitous mug shots and the exterior takes of the ambulance leaving the dead rocker's Pasadena residence. Hildy pronounced the assignment completed. Her overused conceptual brain cells delivered a goofy thought about the planned memorial service for Hooch – wouldn't it be funny if everyone left the ceremony before it was concluded.

Her parallel personal project was shaping up. She'd found two more snippets of the man in the crowd and one more possible shot of him as he walked in slow motion through a large open area where concert-goers lounged freely. She was convinced that she was actually viewing David Fallon at the age of nineteen. She decided to keep the disks out instead of relegating them back to storage and to spend some time later reviewing the segments she'd bookmarked.

**The next day**, on a visit with her mother, Hildy told her she had a surprise. Debbie complimented her daughter's work on the Hooch Conrad piece from the news. It had been replayed on the local morning wake-up show and when Debbie spoke to several of her friends that day at lunch she'd proudly announced that her daughter was the "artist" who had put the piece together. Hildy reminded her mom for the umpteenth time that she was more engineer than artist, but Debbie's proud parental concept remained unaltered.

Hildy set up the DVD and positioned the laptop so both she and her mother could see the screen. The edited scenes played completely and Debbie made no comment, no change in her facial expression of unfulfilled anticipation, no sign that she saw anything that Hildy had fully hoped for - expected her to see.

"You didn't see anyone familiar?" Hildy asked in disbelief.

"No, I don't think so. Play it again?"

After two more screenings, Debbie admitted that Hildy would have to draw a picture, she saw nothing or no one that stood out. All Debbie could get from the video was a wistful flashback of herself as a teenager wearing clothes and hairstyles like those onscreen.

Now Hildy doubted her own initial impressions. Surely if this was the man her mother had been married to for twenty-nine years, Debbie would recognize him, whether on sight or by some kind of intuitive connection thing. Could be Hildy had wasted all that time editing images of a stranger, but she wouldn't let it go just yet.

She cued the footage up again and paused it when her dad's face was the most clear. She pointed him out – there behind the face-painted girl – and watched as her mother adjusted her reading glasses to focus on a single time-blurred face out of dozens in the shot.

"Oh! Oh! Is that David? Is that your dad?" Her hands flew to her mouth and her eyes moistened with sentiment.

Hildy misted over in empathy and said quietly, almost reverently, "Well, you'd be the expert on that."

Debbie touched her husband's young face on the screen with her finger, the wedding ring digit. Hildy felt as if she vanished from the room and all that remained were her parents – electronically reunited after seven years. The air in the room softened and filled with reminiscence. The daughter allowed the widowed mother a soundless moment to go wherever these pictures had taken her.

After Debbie had viewed the clips three more times, she shook herself back to the present and listened to Hildy's tale of how this had come to be.

Debbie said, "I never knew he'd attended Monterey Pop. You know I didn't meet him until sixty-nine when we worked together at the restaurant. He was my daddy's worst nightmare – a twenty-one-year-old Vietnam vet dating his sheltered seventeen-year-old daddy's girl. I remember that David was very into music for the first two or three months we dated – unusually so. He could pull song lyrics and band names out of his head like a regular encyclopedia. If I'd met him today, I could nickname him Google." Her whole face smiled.

"Ma, you look seventeen right now," Hildy said with her face propped in her hand like a child enthralled. "So, he never talked about being in San Francisco in sixty-seven?"

"I'm sorry, Hil, I don't recall him saying anything at all about living in or visiting San Francisco that year. Probably because he was drafted that very fall – only a couple of months after that concert – and we know his war experience changed everything. He'd only been back from Vietnam for three months when we met. And even if he did mention the Monterey Pop Festival, it may not have meant anything to me, a Southern girl who loved the Beatles and Sam the Sham and the Pharaohs, sure, but I knew more about beloved authors than favorite bands. Monterey Pop was not as legendary, not as romanticized as Woodstock. Besides, the late sixties were so full of cultural events that this one was merely part of the mélange."

"Wow, I wish I could talk to Daddy right now," replied a reflective Hildy. "For lots of reasons, but now I'm so curious about his early life. I guess I was always okay with knowing so little because of the … you know, his ongoing issues.

But now, to stumble across a piece of his history and have no way to fill in the blanks …"

"My daughter, the reporter," Debbie said with a smile. "I can't help you with details of your dad's life in 1967. He was a lot of fun when I met him in '69 but I could see, or maybe sense, the serious undertones. And of course, within the next several years, the dark side came to dominate. I believe his pain and his tragic memories changed his life. But, you should never doubt that he was a really good guy."

Debbie told her daughter that she wanted some time to think back over the history, maybe look again at her photo albums. They'd talk again about everything after that.

**By the time** he was unintentionally archived on film at the Monterey Pop Festival, David Fallon, an only child, had already been orphaned and taken in by his grandparents until he finished high school. He told the young Debbie that to deal with his loss he'd thrown himself into his high school studies and his new love – music – before deciding to forgo college. His fervor to be a rock star guitar player matched the dreams of many of his peers. He worked odd jobs and fast food which earned him not only a meager, bohemian living, but also a draft ticket to the conflict in Southern Asia. The frustrated musician spent eleven and a half months in Vietnam involved in covert operations that would, ironically, come to sour him on the very music he'd once immersed himself in as a means of sustaining his grief-edged sanity. Eventually, the songs and bands he'd once revered and emulated became a soundtrack to his wakeful nightmare in Vietnam. The spit-in-his-face non-welcome-back he received on his return home with a naïve assumption that life was as he'd left it sent him reeling with the decisions and difficulties of a life that he'd never planned for. He saw in Debbie a possibility for some scrap of normalcy. Initially suppressing any desire to confess his demons, he was convinced that sharing his inner blackness would likely send her running away from him with his complex issues and search out someone more like herself. But the teenage girl proved a sympathetic, if astounded, listener and friend – eventually much more. David came to believe that she was his own personal second chance at a life and a family. If she wouldn't have him, well, he couldn't see a happy alternative.

Debbie thought about all these things, the few secret, deep places that her beloved but troubled husband had entrusted to her. She concluded that it had to be okay to keep <u>some</u> things between husband and wife, to exclude even a daughter, no matter how curious. Hildy had grown up a witness to her father's fragile constitution, but was only given a basic, general explanation. David had taken his secrets to his grave, and certain ones that he'd shared with Debbie would go with her to her own.

**The interest** in classic rock music that had been nourished in Hildy as she watched the footage of the Monterey Pop Festival took deeper root. The information available to her from the internet and the reference material in the studio's archives fed her hunger for facts and background. She learned more from her mother about the sounds of the revolution, how it felt to be present when this music was in its rowdy toddler stage. The tidbits about David Fallon's early passion for music that slipped into these conversations served to flesh out Hildy's rather one-dimensional memories of her father. In this new infatuation with vintage rock and roll, she felt an affectionate bond with her dad that she'd never known, even before he died. A bittersweet awareness, as it also brought regret at having missed this opportunity while she had a living father.

Debbie insisted, when she and her daughter had these conversations, that Hildy lamented a non-existent missed chance. Debbie explained repeatedly that the war had effectively severed David's single-minded earlier drive toward music. That he'd certainly not have been amenable to sharing this interest with his daughter, that it very well could have pushed him deeper into the dark world that defined his post-war life.

Hildy loved her mother and was growing to respect even more the devotion that she carried for her damaged husband, how difficult their personal relationship must have truly been. But she disagreed wholeheartedly with her mother's insistence on this issue. To Hildy, there was every chance that nurturing this common interest could've made a large difference in her father's mental health – to the good. But this grand experiment in hindsight could never be proved or refuted.

A few days later in a staff meeting at work, Hildy was inspired by some of the free-flowing ideas about upcoming projects at the TV station. She sought out her team leader afterwards and told her that she wanted to run some thoughts by her. Aileen suggested that they get together later that day but Hildy asked for a couple of days to arrange her material in a tighter format. Aileen seemed impressed with the cryptic proposal and told Hildy she looked forward to the unveiling.

The sore neck muscles that habitually resulted from Hildy's job were nothing compared to what ensued after twenty hours in high editing gear. First, she had hashed out some issues with her mother and, surprised and pleased with the results, set about to tell one man's story. A sensitive touch with the personal aspects of her father's life coalesced with the recorded material Hildy had put together, merging into the outline of her project. She now had something solid to show her boss.

**Hildy's documentary** was scheduled to air three weeks later on a Tuesday evening – in the half-hour segment available to local programming that followed the local news. Aileen had been sold by Hildy's comment that many of David Fallon's contemporaries would relate to the story's subject matter. She had pressed for an earlier air date, to more directly benefit from the tie-in that Hooch Conrad had unwittingly provided. But Hildy had begged for adequate editing time, not willing to sacrifice quality and accuracy for expediency.

Hildy and Debbie were together for the premiere, but they'd both seen the finished product several times. They had shunned the invitations from their close friends to have a watch party, preferring a private viewing. Mother and daughter wanted to share the public maiden voyage of this very personal project exclusively with each other.

**As she watched,** Debbie naturally related to the deeply personal aspects of the project, but Hildy had taken painstaking care to protect her father's most private challenges, those that were strictly not for public consumption. Not only was there no hint of exploitation, the talented daughter had created a positive, loving tribute to the father she quite possibly knew better now than ever before. Debbie delighted in the musical aspects of the piece. After all, they were a large part of her history as well.

The final credits rolled and mother and daughter clapped and whooped at each listing of Hildy Fallon's name. They fell into each other's arms in an emotional heap, weeping until the phones started ringing. They spoke to congratulatory friends and family until they each had to beg for mercy, pleading the lateness of the hour.

Both women slept the sleep that comes with relief and release.

**Hildy arrived** at the TV station the next morning to accept applause, and accolades both sincere and campy. A full voice-mail box and forty-seven new emails would take her the better part of the morning to wade through. Most of the messages were from friends or colleagues and ran the gamut from formal and congratulatory to silly. She was addressed as Ms. Memoir and Rockumentary Queen. One message from a former college roommate asked her what she planned to wear to collect her Emmy.

But the most noteworthy, serendipitous communication of all had been forwarded to her from the station's general email address. It read:

Thank you so much for the very moving documentary, *Monterey Papa*.

I thought you may be interested to know that I also appeared in the concert audience sitting near David Fallon. That's me with the **I LUV YOU** on my face. I didn't know David, but after watching your glowing tribute to him, I wish I had.

Thank you again for a well-done, interesting program and my husband and I hope you give us more of the same.

Mary Harmseth Dulles (a.k.a. "Harmony" back in the day) ha.

☻☮☻

# The Earrings

*Sadly, a story that <u>could</u> be true.
It was published in
<u>Still Crazy Literary Magazine</u>.*

Amid a luxurious yawn that extended to her toes and fingertips, Anya noticed the pair of earrings lying next to last night's wine glass on the end table. Not good, taking off her jewelry while relaxing in the living room. How many pairs of earrings were reduced to solitaires because of her bad habit? There was a slightly smudged lipstick mark on the rim of the wine glass and she smiled as she thought that *Red Velvet* looked better on the glass than it had on her lips. She scooped up the turquoise earrings and then the glass, all in one hand, and headed for the kitchen.

When the coffee was ready, Anya filled a fresh mug that had *Viva la Java* imprinted on it. The morning sun made every effort to make acquaintance with her drowsy eyes, but the vast, ancient oak tree in the yard allowed for only a dappled effect on the west wall of the dining room. As a child she had romped in this space and marveled at the movement of light that the rising sun painted there. It occurred to her today that the architect may have designed the structure so as to capture this specific look. Maybe her mother would recall. Well, well, wasn't her mind meandering all over hill and dale today?

As the hazlenut-laced caffeine kicked in she began to feel less fuzzy; the blanks filled in. She *should* be making a plan for today's activities instead of re-living days from forty years ago. In fact, they had an appointment today with a geriatric Alzheimer's specialist to make plans for her mother's ongoing care. Inger was still in the beginning stages of the dread disease, but Anya was studiously acquainted with the bleak prognosis. Her husband's father had lived with Alzheimer's for nine long years, the last three brutal. Anya was beginning to wonder if this was becoming an inevitable twenty-first century conclusion to a long, otherwise fruitful life. Several of her friends and family members were dealing with the disease at one level or another. Was there an epidemic or what?

Inger entered the room then; Anya noted with surprise that her mother had already dressed for the day. Anya said, "Good morning! Don't we look nice?"

"I've not gone around the bend just yet, Anya. I may not be able to manage my checkbook or keep track of my car keys, but I can still dress myself." The elder woman was understandably bitter over this insufferable nightmare that had befallen her and regularly expressed this verdict to Anya. Hadn't she been so careful to exercise her mind, to keep challenging herself even though she would have been justified in choosing to relax and tolerate the inevitable? Inger took the diagnosis personally, believing it to be unjust and undignified.

For Anya, combating her mother's heart-breaking reaction to the diagnosis was more grueling than the struggle to keep an eagle-eye on the everyday affairs of the household, and it was growing more and more difficult to put on her own happy face. After all, she was devastated, too.

Anya sighed and responded to Inger's scolding, "Well, of course you can dress yourself. It seems you have a little more trouble accepting a simple compliment. Anyway, do we need to do anything here this morning? Before the doctor's appointment?"

Inger drew a written list out of her skirt pocket. She raised her head to better focus on the lettering through her bifocals, and moved her lips as she silently read the three items she had thought of last evening as she waited for sleep. In her battle strategy for this disease, she had capitulated to list-making, a habit she was formerly proud to avoid. "Hmm, no, nothing here about the house. A couple of other things, though. I want to drop off some books at the library, and James' birthday is next week. We should try to find something nice for him," she said with obvious pride at her vigilant competence, but also with something like relief. Even a small victory was hard won.

"Okay, good. Come sit here and tell me about this room. Did the architect know about the charming artwork he was creating on these walls? I've always loved the play of the eastern sun in here. I made coffee and juice?"

"I'll get a cup of that coffee," Inger said, smiling suddenly. "How about a cinnamon bun?" As she prepared two warm, aromatic pastries for the two of them, she said, "I've never told you that story? I would've thought you'd heard it many times."

"I know, that's what I thought. But, no, I don't think so."

"Well, his name was H.R. Bonét – the architect, that is. Your uncle James recommended him right after we moved to town. Remember that little duplex we lived in for a few months? Or were you a bit too wee? Anyway, H.R. came out to see the site and started talking all this artistic gibberish about elevation and exposure and, no kidding, he even walked across the street and peered through framed thumbs and forefingers. We did cast a few sidelong glances at him over all that fluff. We merely wanted our dream house to be built on this lot. But we came to learn the value of his expertise. This dining room has always attracted our visitors. And you're right – it's the sunlight." Inger looked dreamily out the large window and sipped coffee.

"Bonét? Was he French?" asked Anya, happy to be in an area of conversation where her mother was presented a chance to showcase her former self-assurance.

"Well, that's what *I* wanted to know. I asked James what we needed with a fancy-schmancy foreigner designing our house, and he said that Monsieur Bonét was as American as Little Rock. That's just the way he put it. And sure enough, Mr. Bonét was not only American, but Southern to boot. His folks had come over from Montpelier,

France right after they married . . . but that's a story for another time."

Anya had gotten up to clear the table. She felt a tentative optimism that this may turn out to be one of her mother's good days.

"Dear, you've left these lovely turquoise …" The word refused to come and a large cavity formed in the optimism Anya had tentatively permitted. After several seconds Inger's eyes misted.

"It's okay, Mother," Anya said gently as she patted the elder woman's age-spotted hand. When had her mother turned into an old woman? "Earrings."

"Yes, of course," her mother recovered, dabbing at her right eye. "Well, I'd best be getting ready for our appointment." Then she looked down and observed that she was already fully dressed.

Anya was quick with a distraction. "Hey, remember when we bought those earrings in Colorado?" She could count on the fact that her mother's long-term memory was in far better condition than her recall from only thirty seconds before.

The technique worked and Inger smiled, expressing a swift parade of three emotions that the ever watchful caregiver recognized. First gratitude, then peace followed by confident recall. Now she bore more resemblance to the mother from another day. "You just *had* to have that pair of earrings. We saw them in the hotel gift shop and I told you to walk around the block and see if the desire remained as strong. Must've been a wise purchase. You still wear them."

"Yup, I've spent more on other jewelry, but I don't feel the same way about any other pieces."

"Remember how they were wrapped in that pink tissue paper?" asked her mother. "When you weren't wearing them, you were gazing at them like they were precious treasure. That tissue paper ended up in ragged strips from being manhandled so many times."

"Hey, I was thirteen," Anya said defensively. "Those were my first 'dangly' earrings. So I was a little squirrely."

"Your father didn't like you in such grown-up jewelry, did he?" Inger folded her arms and set her jaw in imitation of her late husband's infrequent decrees.

Anya laughed out loud. "He actually said he was worried that I'd catch them on a tree limb and tear an ear off. I told him and told him that turquoise hoop earrings were not proper adornment for a trip to the forest, that I'd be sure to wear my diamond safety studs for that."

Inger dissolved into laughter. "You know, he always secretly admired your sense of humor. He called it 'sophisticated.' I'd usually respond that it could sound more like sarcastic sass, if you asked me, but I was just as proud that you could think so quickly."

"Remember that argument we had when I was about fifteen and you called me Sassy Sasserton?" asked Anya through chortles. "Who was the quicker thinker that time?"

"Okay so I won that one," Inger responded as she stood to get a tissue to collect the tears of spontaneous laughter. "But your teenaged years weren't *always* filled with admirable cleverness."

"I know. And if I don't say it enough, thank you for putting up with me. Mothers who survive teenagers should get medals … or awards … or tiaras." Anya smiled as she mimed the placement of a crown on her mother's head.

Anya was surprised by her mother's response to this light-hearted action. Inger wilted slightly and her smile drooped. She said to her daughter, "Well. I guess you're the one who has to earn the crown now, hmm?" Her eyes seemed to reflect her autobiography. "And if I don't remember to tell you, thank you for being here for me. I love you."

Mother and daughter hugged emotionally, each trying to banish the lump from her throat. Anya released her mother and said with as much faux cheer as she could summon, "Okay. Let me just go and put myself together and we'll be ready to leave. I'll have to find something to wear that matches these earrings!"

Inger stood, smoothed her skirt and smiled as with a memory. She said, "Oh, do you remember when we bought those?"

☻☮☻

# To Write, Perchance to Dream

*A mostly true story that I went a little silly with.*

*This story was published in*
<u>*Calliope, A Writer's Workshop by Mail*</u>,
*a publication of American Mensa, Ltd.*

One modern feature of my circa 1950s weekend rental cabin was its wooden deck and walkway. By contrast, age had softened the building's edges; atmospheric humidity had mossed its external shell. The interior's surfaces – floors, walls, ceilings – were all highly varnished plywood, the poor man's paneling. I began to feel I was sheltered in a humbly furnished shipping crate before I got a glimpse of the view from the rear picture window. The river was a living mural, visible between leggy, foliage-rich trees. It flowed lazily beneath a wafting layer of foggy mist that, frankly, was the top reason I had chosen this locale for a cabin getaway. I always felt rather like I was in a fairy tale (one of the stories *without* trolls) when I was able to spend any time in this serenely inspirational area. Tailor-made writer's retreat.

I unpacked the few basics I couldn't leave home without – clothes, computer and cookies – and then left my rental shipping crate to explore the deck that extended out over the water. As I stood inches above the frigid, trout-rich water, a reflexive, subterranean breath of utter relaxation expelled the dregs of stress that clung to me. Already captured by the river's siren song, I sat in one of the sun-tortured plastic chairs on the deck. I saw a trout jump out of the water making a little arc in the air. It was as if he said "Welcome! Enjoy!" and I smiled, charmed. I mentally launched into the words I would use if I were writing this scene since I had actually come here to flex my flabby writer's muscles. But I was determined to also squeeze in a little R & R. Write a little, play a little. A girl's gotta have fun.

So I took frequent breaks outside, enjoying the postcard view and its accompanying ambiance. There the river, there a large white bird gliding gracefully, there a nut falling from a tree for what seemed like hours to finally reach the sloping ground, there the filigree pattern of the sun shining through rippling leaves, there a man's voice from behind me . . . HUH?

"Howdy! How're y'all?" he asked, as if we were standing in line at the market.

Startled, I turned to see a smiling male holding a can of Mountain Dew in one hand and a cigarette in the other. He had an eye condition that caused the left one to wander while the right eye was trained on me. Ostensibly he could view both the river to the southeast and me, westward, simultaneously. He gave off no menacing vibes but, then again, he *had* taken the liberty of inviting himself to cross a privacy fence between cabins.

He asked me where "we" were from and I hastily edited my natural reply of speaking as an individual, here alone. For all he knew, I had a hefty, reclusive, weight-lifting hubby inside the cabin gobbling raw meat and watching that Smackdown show on TV, at the ready to storm out here and re-arrange this intruder's anatomy if I merely whimpered. So I replaced each "I" with "we" and let him draw his own conclusions.

My impudent visitor commented that he and his group had planned an outing for the day and then he would return to his home about eighty miles away. I relaxed a bit when he said it was nice talking to me and turned to go; it appeared that he was lodged in the cabin next door and had merely made an awkward attempt at being neighborly. My mischief-alert meter eased, reset to zero.

I went inside to my computer and after a couple of hours I heard a loud motor outside. From the front window I saw overly-friendly-neighbor-dude exiting in his candy-apple-red pickup truck, each tire bigger than an entire VW Beetle. *ROWDY*, read his vanity license plate. At this point I was caught between two reactions. My visceral sense was of inadvertently landing in a real-life sequel to the movie *Deliverance*. But from my head I heard, "Forsooth – you're at a story farm. Harvest!" (I really hate it when my very own brain utters pompous things like *forsooth*. Apparently my muse for this project was intoning William Shakespeare or Frasier Crane.)

I submissively began a rough draft, and later went outdoors for another break. From near Howdy Rowdy's cabin came the sound of large barking dogs–judging by their bass tones, no French Poodles or Pomeranians, they. I hoped they were chained or otherwise confined because I saw no humans and heard no one call out to shush the persistently vocal dogs.

With my quasi-protagonists off property being tourists, my keyboard lay dormant. Should I forge ahead or wait until another serendipitous real-life event played itself out, self-propelling the story onward? I'd had no clue in advance that my writing retreat weekend would be augmented by real-time events, complete with unique characters no less. So shouldn't I take advantage of that gift? I decided to work on other incomplete projects until this one demanded my return. No doubt, Frasier or Willy would nag me back to this particular Word document at some point.

Later, as I sat in my room-with-a-view enjoying an officially-sanctioned chick food lunch of fruit and yogurt, I heard Rowdy's dogs, now affectionately dubbed Brutus and Killer, barking frantically. They had raised the volume and intensity enough to renew my interest and I went out to scan the area for a cause. Ah, up the river came a gaggle of geese floating/paddling in an unstructured line. Honking loudly, they were the likely cause of the uproar from Brutus and Killer who were now agitated enough to be straining at their chains, if my hearing was accurate. Thankfully, they soon gave up the boisterous but ineffective struggle and I stood out over the river watching the birds while picturing their webbed feet encased in square, cartoon ice cubes when they tried to exit the cold, cold trout stream.

Still later, I was relaxing with a glass of white wine that was surprisingly but pleasantly acidic (Yo, Frasier, give it a rest). I put on an Eagles CD, closed my eyes and welcomed a peaceful, easy feeling. I was moved to accompany the band on air drums and I gave over to music-borne nostalgia. Presently, I wandered down to the river deck again to soak up as much of nature's peace as I could hold. While I stood quietly leaning on the deck rail, I watched a beaver as it dog-paddled (beaver-paddled?) to cross the river. I don't know if beavers have genetically poor eyesight but this unfortunate creature repeatedly ricocheted off trees and logs as though blind or lost.

By late afternoon, with no further plot development from next door, I took myself into town for an Oriental buffet feast of spicy kung pao shrimp and General Tso's chicken.

That evening I soaked in the candle-lit spa tub filled with girly-scented bath salts, and then I put myself to bed hoping to rise early enough to compose a story ending. As things turned out, Mr. Sandman visited with a doozy of a finale.

On this night after a day spent judging every occurrence by its fictional potential, I dreamed: I pack my car and try to leave for home on Sunday morning, but Rowdy's monster truck is blocking my way. He stands outside my car door with his arms folded defiantly and sings (badly) a mish-mash of Eagles' song lyrics, *"You can check out any time you like, but you can never leave. I'm brutally handsome and you're terminally pretty - let's go live life in the fast lane."* He smiles maniacally and leers at me with his western eye and over at Killer and Brutus with the other. This is apparently their cue to commence playing dueling air banjos while making rumbly musical sounds with Scooby Doo-esque vocals – ROO ROO ROO, roo roo ... I hear geese honking and steal a look back at the river to see a beaver attempting to swim around a goose but he keeps blindly plowing into it, causing the goose to be all feathers and flapping and fussing. Next, up pops a trout singing *Don't Worry, Be Happy* as he arcs gracefully out of the water again and again, sometimes the "*Happy*" sounding a bit gurgle-y as he hits the water prematurely. Finally, a genuine Brothers Grimm troll steps out from beneath the river deck and strolls toward me. All other action stops as he calmly, wisely, tells me from behind ZZ Top whiskers that this is all merely a "conceptual consequence" of the spicy Oriental food. I was to take two antacids and call him in the morning.

The End. Fade Out. Wake up.

Whew! Methinks I stumbled upon the gastronomic inspiration secret of writers Stephen King and J.K. Rowling.

😎 ☮ 😎

# Dream Analysis, Hollywood Style

*I actually did have this dream years ago.
It was odd that I retained it, as I usually don't recall dreams.*

I dreamed about doors.
Not a *Come on baby light my fire* kind of Door, but literal entries and exits. I'd fallen asleep after a leisurely evening of television and had managed to sleep soundly for the remainder of the night. This dream occurred at dawn's earliest light, else it would certainly have been gone with the wind, since my nocturnal dramas usually flee without a trace at the cessation of the REMs. I mean, Ebenezer Scrooge's dream was a doozy of a morality tale for the ages, as was Bob Newhart's classic sitcom-ending dream that brilliantly tied into his former series.

So, this preserved dream was a rarity and I mused over it after snatching at the retreating dregs of ethereal detail. Cue the wavy-edged effects ~~~ In the medical center where I work, I had just left the Mental Health Unit and then remembered something that caused me to try to return. But I discovered I'd forgotten the key code that would unlock the secured doors. I went to each door (infuriatingly, there were several more dream doors than real-life ones), but I was still shut out and found no one to ask for help. Frustrated, I turned and went through a door marked *Maintenance*, only to encounter set after set of double doors, each subsequent pair different in style from the last. I felt like Agent Maxwell Smart, endlessly navigating the Top Secret access to C.O.N.T.R.O.L. headquarters. I remember feeling tangibly discouraged, and I never progressed through a single door.

That's it – The End. Fade out. It's a wrap. No complicated plots, no horrors of discovering I've worn jammies, or my birthday suit to school, no morphing into other characters or personalities mid-dream, no dearly departed loved ones delivering a timely message from Beyond, no clichéd falling or flying. Just a lingering curiosity about the meaning of doors as the starring characters of one dream. I am not a medical or psychiatric professional, but I would venture an amateur opinion that doors almost certainly rank high in symbolism under the category: The Stuff That Dreams are Made Of.

After frustrating, ineffective attempts at D.I.Y. dream analysis, I felt rather like I had after watching the anticlimactic *Seinfeld* series finale – as if the show would return again after one last squillion-dollar commercial to knock my socks off with the ending to end all endings. I like clear and tidy conclusions (even from a show about nothing). I want the end to aptly justify the means. I need that light bulb moment. Even an imagination as active as mine still craves closure, as provided by the author. I don't like to read fiction where I am left to supply my own ending – isn't that the author's job? Me? I was taught to finish what I start.

So, awake, I start by exploring the likely meaning of a single door in my dream – the one marked *Maintenance*. Hmm. Even if that does point to the final significance, I remain puzzled. Am I to *maintain* status quo? Or should I be open and ready to recognize and repair some dysfunctional facet or issue in my life? Am I to put my car in the shop for an oil change? Call the janitor?

Pulling out for a wider shot, should I re-think a daunting new avenue I had recently and tentatively pursued; a risky opportunity that had proven, to date, to be the proverbial succession of closed doors? Or have I accidentally-on-purpose jumbled the key code on my own "doors," leaving my life's dream without a clear path to realization? Could a uniformed Jack Nicholson justifiably snarl at me: "You can't handle the doors!"? Is there a clue in the fact that the dream involves the *Mental Health* Unit as opposed to the Cardiac Floor, the Surgical Ward or the Emergency Room?

Is it possible that the dream's directive is less cerebral, more practical or fiscal, like the investment guy who advised a young Dustin Hoffman in *The Graduate*?

Dream: "I've got one word for you – Doors."

Could it be a fortune cookie-esque advisory: "Always remember the key code or you'll embark on a long, dark, wearisome journey that ends nowhere?"

Oh, for the professional (but droll) expertise of TV docs Frasier Crane and Bob Hartley. Or ... hey! ... maybe I should call the quintessential authority on opening doors. Monty Hall, can you hear me? I've got a boiled egg and a garden rake in my purse ... 😎☮😎

# We Should Have Seen It Coming

*This is a true account of the events of one afternoon several years ago. I was invited to read the tale on the radio (NPR) on a program produced in North Little Rock, Arkansas called Tales from the South.*

A new fishing boat! Well, new to us anyway. The old boat had died a slow death when finally the plug was pulled due to the diagnosis of terminal Hole-in-Bottomitis. One too many rocks in the generator-lowered White River had ended a long, fruitful life and a replacement boat of different style and dimensions was fitted out for the maiden voyage.

The initial trip with my husband's friend had yielded the first necessary alteration, something-something-blah-blah about the motor's position in the water. Don't ask me, I'm not nautical .... at all. I don't know port from a porthole. So that fix was carefully and mathematically applied by my proficient husband and his equally skilled friend.

Two days later I was excited about taking the newly modified boat out on the White River with a side trip to the mouth of the Buffalo River to a spot that is very meaningful to my husband Wayne and I - he took me there on our second date, a mere 3 ½ years ago. It was quite a romantic visit that day, much as the ensuing relationship has been, but that's a story for another day.

So, we backed the boat trailer down the ramp, stopping just so, to unhitch and launch the boat. Wayne, wearing old tennis shoes that would have been more suited as impromptu skates on a frozen lake, lost his footing and slipped completely into the frigid trout river for an accidental dip. He was fine, if chilled and embarrassed, but maybe we should have seen the portent of the slip and fall.

He launched the boat and gave me the signal to pull vehicle and trailer up into the parking lot. Aye Aye Skipper. But all of a sudden he was up there with me, shouting for me to get back in the SUV, he'd left the plug out of the boat and it was taking on water. We speedily backed down, rescued the boat and drained it before employing the plug. Wayne gave the motor a turn before launching again, and got silence for his effort. Ahhhh, the battery wires had not been reconnected. Hmmmmmm, maybe we should have allowed just a wee bit of suspicion at this point.

Upon re-launch, Wayne neglected to disconnect the winched cable that held the boat firm to the trailer. By this time, a group of others who had been milling around the area apparently felt the need to helpfully intervene - possibly believing this to be our very first rodeo, and who could blame them if they'd witnessed Wayne's fall and then the sinking boat? Wayne figured out the cable problem and remedied it before outside help would have been just plain embarrassing for a man who had fished and boated this river for decades.

So, boat plugged and launched, my job was to park the vehicle and trailer which I handled quite proficiently, thank you, and proceeded to lock up our personal belongings with a supposed spare key in my hand. Only ... it wasn't. A spare key to *that* car, anyway. Noticing a back window slightly down, I went to unlock the door to raise the window, whereupon I discovered the spare key's refusal to magically morph from a Jeep key to a Ford key. I waved to Wayne who pulled the boat up onshore and came to help. Since he had left his own keys and wallet safely in the car, we had to improvise. A tree branch was fashioned into a primitive Slim Jim to manipulate the automatic door lock from the slightly open window and we were back in business. But by now, we really should have been prepared for ... more.

Wayne turned to walk back down to the boat. I heard him say, "Oh no!" just before he launched hisownself toward the river. Yup, you can guess that the boat had loosened itself in the river's current and had begun our boat ride down the river, sans passengers. Flinging off shirt and glasses, Wayne dove in, sorta like they used to do on Baywatch? Now, for those who don't know, the White River is NO swimmin' hole. **Nobody**, except possibly polar bears or penguins, would visit this trout Mecca for the purpose of recreational bathing, any more than you would the Arctic Sea or the moon's Sea of Tranquility.

A 20-yard Australian-crawl-sprint reclaimed the boat. Wayne lobbed his blueing arms over the side and after a minute or two to gather his breath (he's in good shape, but not for a spot on the Olympic team), he hoisted his right leg to the inside to laboriously re-board the errant vessel, only to be immediately advised by 3 fishermen in an approaching boat that they had headed over to rescue the boat themselves. This would have been a much saner and <u>way</u> more temperate solution.

This still wouldn't be the last misstep.

One unintentionally wet boat pilot and his dry – so far – bride finally set out to enjoy a boat ride meant to recreate a romantic bygone day, down the White River from Buffalo City to just beyond the spot where it meets the beautiful Buffalo River. There is an archaic but very scenic bridge support built from stacked rocks, a place Wayne had taken me on our second date. Recently we have become bridge hunters and decided we wanted a photo of this handsome structure, which had, unbeknownst to an acquainting couple, become the very first bridge in our collection. Awww.

All went well until we approached a shallow rapids passageway and Wayne strategically chose the spot that appeared to be the deepest and easiest traversed. A few yards out, from my position in a boat seat in the front of the boat, I saw the hazard and gave an alert, but not nearly soon enough. We high-centered on a sneaky, boat-grabbing boulder, cleverly camouflaged by the rushing water. Momentum pulled my unfastened seat to the left and, impossibly, I watched the river rapids rise up to meet me as I flipped over on all fours to plunge torso first into the glacial gush. Gifted with fairly good reflexes, I rebounded to my feet, gasping while retrieving the ability to breathe. Wayne had exited the boat and was holding on to steady it with his right hand while reaching out his left to save me from being swept away. Profuse and sincere apologies were the soundtrack I heard as I coaxed my dazed lungs into survival mode. A quick assessment revealed both of us to be sound, and I was somehow able to swiftly process the ridiculous sequence of events to begin laughing deeply until I noted an announcement from my legs that they had been plunged in the 55 degree water plenty long enough and would I mind curbing my enthusiasm to GET BACK IN THE BOAT!?

Reboarding the boat – Wayne's second time that day – we continued on, me helplessly giggling as I relived the improbable scene over and over. I was fully clothed, intending to change into swimwear when we arrived at the much more temperate Buffalo River site. The breezy ride was invigoratingly chilly but I hardly noticed it, guffawing as I was at the succession of Lucy & Ethel, Jim Carrey, Inspector Clouseau events of the past few minutes.

Things finally became calmer and less chaotic after this. We got one more surprise, but this one was welcome – a reward or consolation prize from above. As we lounged in the swimmer-friendly, bathtub-balmy waters of the Buffalo

River, we noted the abrupt presence of a stunning bald eagle, swooping from the sky for a fishing expedition. We watched his graceful attempt and then marveled as he elegantly spiraled the thermals down river. What serendipity!

We did get our coveted bridge photo, and enjoyed a memorable revisit of our second date without further channeling the 3 Stooges. My sweet husband opined that it was good that the wacky high jinks of this nostalgia trip had not occurred during our initial acquainting boat ride 3 years earlier, as it most certainly could have been a relationship deal-breaker.

But I don't agree at all. **I** believe we would merely have been telling this story for 3 years longer. Only next time… I check the plug, the battery, the spare car key, the winch hook, the anchor, and our life insurance policies first!

😎☮😎

# STILL WONDERING, AFTER ALL THESE YEARS

*This contemplative piece is a diversion
from the other, light-hearted works.*

    I received a forwarded email that contained a wise missive: There are always reasons why certain people in our past don't make it into our present. A deep thought, of far more use than those alarming emails that warn about the dangers of soda or plastic.
    I can look through my high school yearbooks and be unable to recollect some of the faces recorded on those thick, shiny pages, but there are others who earned a permanent spot in my recall. One of my closest childhood friends (I'll call her Jane) was killed in a vehicle accident in 1975 at the age of 21. At that busy stage of young adulthood, we were not as close as we had been through high school and the short years immediately thereafter - our married lives led us onto different paths. But our expanded group of two

husbands and three children socialized occasionally and I've missed her very much through the years.

Jane had been a trusted confidant during those explosive years of adolescence in the 1960s. I can remember us as dramatic teenagers, sitting in the shadowy attic of her house, asking the Ouija board solemn questions about our uncertain, scary, exciting futures. We were high school cheerleaders together and worked at the same drive-in restaurant. We shared a love of the band The Guess Who, but differed on other musical tastes – I preferred the big sounds of rock; her faves were the smoother, lesser-volumed Carole King and Simon & Garfunkel. Today, decades later, when I hear an old song from those more introspective musicians I think of Jane and wonder how she would feel to know that I've grown to appreciate those songs and their sentiments on their own merits.

Other fundamental differences between us have become more evident from my present perspective. She appreciated the more artistic side of life; I can remember believing that the word "artist" described only painters of pictures. She was mildly interested in the paranormal; I thought it merely an invention of science-fiction writers and Hollywood. She was free-thinking and expressive in her personal style, her attire; I wanted to look like everyone else, or at least the cool everyone elses. She was far braver about taking risks than I who was afraid of even the possibility of pain or failure. But for a few years, the mixture of our commonalities and contrasts made for good chemistry.

I've wondered many times if Jane had an inkling about her untimely death. I'd seen her a few days before she died, and I sensed that she didn't seem quite herself. I left her house with an uneasy feeling that I had no reference or experience to help me define. But from an even earlier time, was it possible that she had some form of subliminal understanding and as a result, experienced accelerated stages of human development? Not to say that she was *always* mature and well-adjusted – we'd had a silly feud in the 8$^{th}$ grade over a boy, and she seriously wounded my feelings with a choice she made about her wedding.

I can't say why, but I often use Jane as a sort of benchmark for the comparison between the world in 1975 and these many subsequent years – much in the way people time-date their lives around a traumatic event such as a war or a house fire. I frequently wonder how she would view the many things that didn't exist or were vastly different in her day. Even in the surreal atmosphere of her funeral I ached to go to her afterwards and share my thoughts on the event and the participants, as I would have for any other occasion in our common experience. I lost my 75-year-old grandpa a few months after Jane but I mourned my peer's passing on a much deeper level than his.

In the parameters of my fantasy, I apparently assume that Jane had been kept in a celestial isolation booth since February 1975, making the occasion of her unprecedented return to life as an alien unfamiliar with modern times. While we shared a very similar small-town genesis, she has not lived with and witnessed the day-to-day, minute-by-minute warp-speed evolution of our world as I have. What reaction would she have to personal computers, cell phones, streaming music, internet, 9-11, Covid, climate change and a deeply divided political America? What would her opinions be about the current economy, youth culture and morality?

The city where Jane and I grew up is radically altered, both in population and attitude, so much so that it regularly ranks high on those lists where urban/population growth statistics are calculated. Jane would barely recognize this twenty-first century version of her hometown. If she *were* able to reappear, how would it feel to know she has a grandchild, having not lived past her daughter's age of eighteen-months? What would Jane say about the monumental changes in the health-care industry, one that she was studying to enter when she died? Would she smile knowingly to learn that I had grown much more spiritually inclined, and much braver about risk-taking, even with my wardrobe? How amused would she be to know that my sensibilities have morphed so that a classic Carole King lyric gave me words to help illustrate and define the painful breakup of my marriage, or that the nuances and harmonies in a Simon and Garfunkel song can now take me to my happy place?

After receiving answers to those questions and more, I'd report to Jane about the realities of living life on earth during the distinctive decades since her death. I'd have to tell her that the Ouija board had, in the end, been a useless tool to accurately predict our lives, that a mere toy could in no way prepare us for the difficulties, tragedies, joys and discoveries that every human faces as we age. I would tell her that she'd missed out on a lot of great things, but conversely, she'd been spared heartache, turmoil and fear on both societal and personal levels.

I am so happy to have had Jane in my life - however briefly - and I cannot know why she was taken at the age of 21. True to that wise email I received, along with my faith in God, I know there is good reason. No doubt many lives have been altered to some degree due to her loss – I read somewhere that situations can be affected by either the presence OR the absence of any particular person or thing. Heavy stuff. Impenetrable.

I would enjoy conversing with someone who is not inured, not steeped in the hodgepodge of history that composes our world, not grown cynical or numb or oblivious. Maybe a non-participant to the last 5 decades, having untouched sensibilities and outlook, could cast some measure of objective logic and enlightenment on how the world has changed since 1975. While I recognize that every generation looks back toward childhood with a personalized combination of nostalgia, wonder and bewilderment, surely the Baby Boomers who cast that backward glance have a disproportionately wide gap between the mores, habits and norms of our mid-century coming-of-age and this hyper-advanced yet baffling New Millennium.

>>><<<

# Conway Stories

The following stories pay homage to the small city in Arkansas where I grew up. Experiencing the mid-century societal revolution in such a place truly shaped me.

# Window Shopping

*Hard to recall here in the new millennium, but in mid-century Conway, youngsters could safely stroll the streets ... after dark.*

Every time I went to Ceely's house, it smelled like cooked mushrooms. I didn't know until I was an adult that the distinctive aroma was mushrooms, though, since I was trained to avoid asking rude questions (or innocent questions that could be considered rude). In my childhood, the only contact I had with culinary mushrooms was the diced variety contained in cream of mushroom soup, a key ingredient in tuna casserole which was a family staple.

    The occasion for my olfactory mystery being solved in adulthood had been a date with a guy who cooked dinner for me. He'd looked at me from behind his sauté pan like I was kookoo when I'd blurted, "That's it! That's Ceely's house!"

Back on this summer Friday night, 4 of my 6th grade classmates and I were to gather at Ceely Donohue's house to "bunk" in her basement. Of course, we all knew Bunking Party Rule Numero Uno: **Abandon all hopes of actual sleep. We can sleep when we're dead**.

After stuffing ourselves with Fritos and Rotel cheese dip and discussing merits and drawbacks of every boy we'd ever had a crush on, comparing favorite TV shows and cartoons (Jetsons won the cartoon category, Petticoat Junction and Dr. Kildare tied for first in the live action category) and giggling ourselves to tears over goofy, nonsensical jokes, LuAnn suggested we take a walk. Ceely had to let her dad know we were leaving for a bit and we were off on a dusky dark walk toward downtown, a couple of blocks distant.

On this 1965 June evening we were at various points on our awkward but buoyant adolescent journey. On the cusp of seventh grade, any level of being out and away from our families felt like sweet freedom to us. We skipped, trotted and strolled along the streets of the neighborhood. Once, Angie and I actually did a dramatic imitation of a tango we'd seen in a movie, setting off the group giggles again, but at this point in the party, I could've recited the pledge of allegiance and gotten the same response.

The change in atmosphere of a deserted shopping area was the first impression I noted while approaching a darkened section of downtown that I usually visited only during busy shopping hours that, on most days, ended about 5pm. The ethereal effect of the stores' security lighting on the sidewalks and streets made me feel as though I'd left my familiar town and visited a foreign one.

In the window of Dayer's Jewelry, we each chose our future engagement rings while discussing the style our wedding gowns would be. The Western Auto Store's windows were full of all manner of household and toy items, many of which elicited hilarious stories of family foibles. Jennie could barely relate the tale of her little brother's goofy accident on a tricycle that had occurred when he hit the family's snoozing German Shepherd. [Note: No toddlers or animals were harmed in the creation of this story.]

Heiliger's Book Store's window was tiny, to match the wee paper-and-ink scented space that seemed to somehow contain every book we couldn't get at the Faulkner County Library. The MAD Magazine (What, me worry?), cards, gifts, and impenetrable poetry books were a huge draw for my sister and me. I also loved to browse the stationery selection, though my only letters during that time were to a pen pal from Morrilton that our teacher had arranged for each of us. (Dear Fran, How are you? I am fine.)

Around 10:00, Mary Sue stopped in front of Greeson's and began a running dialogue with Ceely, pretending to be seated in a soda fountain booth and apparently enjoying a snack of cherry phosphates and greasy French fries.

Mary Sue, suddenly Scarlett O'Hara, said, "Oh dahling, did you hear about Mizz Frizz and her beau?"

Ceely stuffed an invisible French fry into her mouth and chewed cartoonishly while answering, "Oh, do tell ... um, dahling."

I bent over and cracked up at their feigned elegance that was pure feme fatale tinged with a heavy dollop of Southern Sixth Grader.

Mary Sue gave me the stink-eye but then winked as she continued. "Oh, they eloped to Eureka Springs and got married in a haunted hotel!"

Ceely dabbed at her lips with an unseen napkin before replying as an older female who had been around the block a time or two. "Tsk tsk. What a horrid omen for them! Why, on this good earth would they go and do THAT?"

"Well, dear, I heard from Zsa Zsa who got it from Audrey who said that Bette claimed that she couldn't say for sure, mind you, but that a Ouija Board may have been involved in THE. WHOLE. THING." Mary Sue almost didn't get through the sentence in the tragi-serious tone in which she had begun. She stifled giggles.

"Woooo ooooo ooooo," hooted Jennie through hands that formed parentheses around her mouth, lending appropriately spooky music as background.

Ceely's wheels were obviously turning, surely attempting to top this goofy dialogue gauntlet. "FOR REAL????????? Girl, she's just askin' for a world of hurt! Um ... and him too! Well, I do declare, what *some* people will do!"

Jennie kept up the ghostly sound effects, which I thought were getting a little annoying, like she was trying to steal the scene. Inspired, I jumped up and yelled, "Boo!!!"

The spell broken, we all laughed as an adolescent male voice from a passing car yelled, "Hey kiddies! Past your bedtime! Better watch out for the booooooogy man!" He added teen boy yuks that faded as the car raced off.

Jennie shouted after him, "That's so funny I forgot to laugh!"

Ceely chimed in with a whiny, "I know you are but what am I?"

We moved down the street to Ben Franklin's. The only interior light was in the very back of the store above the *Employees Only* door. The store seemed much unlike itself, shadows more prominent than the thousands of bins of baubles and miscellany that were like magnets to kid customers with a few coins to spend.

LuAnn said, "Ooh, I know! Each of us tell something that we got from here. I'll go first. I bought a little blue bottle of Evening in Paris perfume for my mom for Christmas when I was ... 7. It spilled in my mom's purse and she had to throw the bag away after trying everything she could to get the reek out. It WAS naaaaaasty."

I relayed the story of a pink feather boa I'd picked out, buying it with tooth fairy money. I think I was 6 or so, and wore the thing ragged pretending to be a Hollywood starlet. My mom was not happy with the constant "feather" shedding that she made me clean up. She'd say, "Okay, Miss Monroe, it's time to clean up the set."

Jennie said she'd bought a pair of flip flops and a swimming pool floatie (with pictures of a mermaid on it); each had lasted for one trip to Miller's Swim Club. John-John Avery had cannon-balled it while Jennie had been sitting on the side of the pool and "that was all she wrote." She stepped on a pop-top and blew out a flip flop as she ran to tattle to her big sister about John-John's antics.

Mary Sue had chosen baby chicks from the store for 3 years running when she was little. "I always wanted the pink ones. They never lived past a few days. I buried them in the back yard, next to our dog Shoo Shoo Boo Boo Loo Loo."

I said, "Oh I remember her! She was so fluffy and she made those cute little sneeze sounds."

Ceely whistled and quoted Rawhide, "Head 'em up and move 'em out, girls," motioning for us to be on our way back to her house. As she leisurely led the group, she told her own Ben Franklin's story. "When I was about ... 12," she paused here to glance back, checking to see whether we picked up on the fact that she was *currently* 12, "I bought a fabulous brooch for my winter coat here. It had many diamonds, rubies and emeralds and it shined like the sun."

She winked, adding a flourish of hands, as though modeling its placement near her collar bone;

her accent had come to mimic the earlier scene she'd played at Greeson's with Mary Sue. "I wore it to Janie Benson's house when she had a birthday party and missed it when I looked for it later. Then a couple months ago I could've sworn I saw it made into a necklace and hanging around Janie's big brother's girlfriend's neck."

Mary Sue said, "Cee, you should be in the movies, or at least on TV. All the stuff you make up."

"Well, who knows?" Ceely quipped. "It could happen."

By the time we reached Ceely's driveway we were whisper-singing *Can't Buy Me Love*, our fists gripping invisible microphones except for LuAnn who provided percussion ala Ringo.

😎☮😎

## American Graffiti at the Downtown Circle, circa 1969

*This story will test your movie trivia knowledge. A couple of nostalgic films lend character names and a bit of plot to this tale.*

"So, who is the new guy ... in the Falcon, what would you call it, maroon? Purple? Red?" Joey asked.

"Dunno," answered Dan, driving his dad's land-yacht Pontiac. "Hey, did you talk to Steve? He coming tonight?"

"No, he's got a date, but we might still spot him, if they're doing the circle. He owes me five bucks," Joey said. "Keep an eye out. Hey ... chicks at ten o'clock!"

"Who ... oh, that's Eileen Banks. The one driving, anyway."

"Hmm. I heard she moved ... Little Rock or Fort Smith or somewhere," Joey said.

"Well, she must be missin' all the hot guys in Conway, then, cuz there she is, with a carload. When we see them next go-round, let's wave them over, see if they wanna ride," Dan said as he sat up straighter. "Too, I want to stop at Bob & Herb's for a coke."

"Okay, my man, but you better plan a trip to Horton's restroom after that. You know you'll have to."

"Well, '*my man*,' we got time, and the night is young."

"Hey, there's that guy with the new Charger ... in Kroger's lot. I wish I had that car and Tony what's-his-name had a ... a ... roller skate," Joey said.

Dan asked, "He the one always doin' the quarter with whoever shows up with a worthy car?"

"I only heard about one time, but yeah, Tony aced it. Let's hang out for a while. Maybe we'll spot Eileen's car ... and Steve too."

When they parked the car and headed over to join the small crowd admiring the shiny brown '69 Charger, Bernie Coombs yelled a greeting. Standing near the Charger, he had his arm around Nita Ames whose hand clasped his. Bernie's senior ring on her left hand seemed to hold her attention as she blew bubbles with her gum.

Owner of the Charger, Tony and his girl Maria, talked animatedly to a guy in a fastback Mustang while Three Dog Night's *One is the Loneliest Number* soundtracked the scene.

Tony was nodding to Riff Lochlan, driving the Mustang, when Joey and Dan approached the Charger. Maybe the coolest car on the lot, the coolest car in town. Joey was a Dodge man and barely gave the Mustang a second glance, but Dan stood with his hands in his pockets, ping-ponging a covetous gaze to both cars. His lead-sled Pontiac Catalina – or his dad's – was merely transportation. Absolutely no one would pause driving The Circle to come and admire it. One day he'd have a muscle car.

Tony was distracted from his conversation with Riff by the guys admiring his wheels, so he gave Riff a two-fingered salute, patted the Mustang door and turned. Slightly puffing up his chest, Tony said, "Hey, y'all. Nice, huh? I'm handing out hankies to catch all the drool."

Joey shook his head appreciatively. "Too cool for school, man."

Dan said, "What's it got in it?"

"440 Magnum," Tony bragged. Dan couldn't help but envision Tony as an over-the-top Barney Fife when the deputy would annoyingly sniff, adjust his belt and brag.

"Horses?" Joey asked after whistling his admiration.

Tony's chest puffed again; Dan wondered if he might pop a vein as he answered, "375. Heavy-duty clutch. Thinkin' about a cam."

Joey heard his name called and waved off Tony, then pointed at Dan before trotting off to catch Steve Arnholder who had stopped his car just before pulling onto Front Street.

Dan told Tony he'd sure like a ride sometime when Tony had nothin' better to do. "I'm kinda undecided on what kind of wheels I'm gonna want."

Tony said, "Will do. I got a carload tonight."

Dan glanced over to see if Joey had finished dunning Steve and found him sauntering back, his wallet out.

"I'm flush now," Joey said before singing, "You ready to hit the road, Jack?"

They discussed both muscle cars while driving the few blocks to Bob & Herb's drive-in. The lot was full of cars, their occupants standing in groups in the warm night air. From somebody's car radio came the Beatles singing *Yellow Submarine.* Joey spotted Eileen's car. Windows down, the girls were singing along to the Beatles, except for the one sitting shotgun who was talking to James Offrey as he leaned on her window.

"Come on, there's, uh, Eileen," Joey said. "We must be livin' right ... gettin' all our wishes tonight."

Dan took out his comb and tried his hardest to slick himself into James Dean while walking to the other side of the lot.

Eileen had 2 girls with her, though Joey thought he'd counted 4 when he first spotted them. He called out as he approached the passenger side, "Hey kids. What's shakin'?"

James raised up from his stooped position at the window, spotted Joey and Dan and lifted his chin in greeting. He pushed his hair back, widened his stance, and folded his arms.

Joey said, "Hey, ladies, how you doin'? Hey, James."

Dan imitated James' chin salute and said, "What's up?"

"Oh, you know, just drivin' the circle. Hangin' out," Eileen's passenger said.

Joey said, "Far out. Um, Eileen, right? Someone said you moved?"

Eileen sipped her drink and answered, "Yeah, it's a bummer ... my dad's job, and all. I'm spending the weekend with Nancy." She thumbed toward the girl in the back seat and then pointed at the front seat. "This is Alice."

Joey introduced himself and Dan, and then said, "And looks like y'all already know James."

James found his voice and said, "Yeah, Alice and me work together."

Alice added, "Yeah, at Frank Brannon's."

Dan joined in, "Yeah? What would Boss Man Frank say about you hangin' at his rival Bob & Herb's?"

James grinned and answered, "He'd probably say, 'Y'all bring me a cup of black walnut ice cream! He's, like, cool."

Joey started to put the moves on Eileen, thinking the girls would ride with him and Dan, but the sound of a motor revving stole everyone's attention. Tony's Charger was racing south, followed only a bit more tranquilly by Riff in his Mustang. The Bob & Herbs crowd watched the cars zoom until their brake lights lit up at the curve 4 blocks down.

Gradually starting to return to their conversations, now peppered with comments on the racing duo, Steve Arnholder pulled up in the gas station parking lot next door, jumped out of his car and announced, "Hey y'all! Get to the quarter! NOW PLAYING ... Charger v Mustang! Be there!" He actually did sound like the radio commercial guy. All that was missing was the "Sunday! Sunday! Sunday!"

Within 10 minutes, the only car remaining on the fast-food lot was a station wagon containing a family. A poodle in the back seat barked from the open window, either chastising the noisily departing teenagers or wishing he could be a part of the action.

Bob & Herb's night shifters Beth and Pauline expressed dismay that they were going to miss the fun. Pauline tossed a cleaning rag into a chair in the back, saying, "Total bummer."

+++

Maria sighed relief when Tony let off the gas as they approached the drive-in theater. She had already smacked his shoulder when the accelerator neared the floor. Though she loved the groovy sound from the Charger's motor, she did not want to be in the car when Tony was pulled over and ticketed. Nuh uh. She felt okay to roll down the window all the way.

In the back seat, Bernie and Nita had been mostly silent until Nita yelped at the night air rushing in. "Hey!" she said, "The hair? Took me all afternoon to get it to mind me!"

Maria said, "Oh, sorry. Not thinking, I guess."

Bernie addressed Maria, "I thought maybe you were going to cut out! Like, vamoose!" Then he reached over to his date and drew her near. "Aw, Nita girl, you'd be beautiful even without hair!"

Nita gave him her look but kissed him anyway.

Tony's rearview mirror gave him the show in the back seat, causing him to fake throw up. "Blech, y'all. I don't know if you're actually worthy of hanging out in Boss Charger. I may need to be more particular in who I award those seats to. First requirement: Do Not Gross Out the Driver."

"Well, we'll see about all that 'boss Charger' stuff, Richard Petty, you got a challenge coming up."

"Who's got a challenge? Riff's the one who needs to be shakin' all over," Tony sniffed, again mimicking Barney Fife. "His ... *pony* car will be limpin' in shame after this."

Riff was jazzed. His 351 Windsor V8 Mustang would be the victor – and the crowd goes willlllllld!! Ford Wins! First. On. Race. Day!!!!!!!!!!! He pictured himself in the Indy 500 ... zoom ... screeeeeech ... zoooooom .... He launched into a loud but off-key version of *Born to be Wild. Get your motors runnin' ...*

+++

Back at Bob n Herbs, instinct and adrenalin pushed Dan and Joey to race across the parking lot for Dan's Pontiac. They were not going to miss this race, or whatever it was to be. As they cleared the city limits on the way to the Quarter, Joey said, "Ahhhhh. Probably blew it with Eileen and the girls." He smacked the glove box.

"I dig it," Dan sneered, "You want out? Walk back?"

Joey didn't get the obvious chop since he was turned around to check the traffic behind him.

"Hey, the girls are right behind us! Our smooth moves musta worked."

"What ... the two words we got out? That's a whole lotta 'smooth' per word, ain't it? You're dreamin'. They probably just want to see the show."

Joey began a snarky comeback, but then got a glimpse of Eileen's car passing them. Alice's window was down and she blew them a kiss. From the back seat, Nancy had her window down too, yelling gleefully, "Neener Neener Neener!"

Joey fell a little bit in love ... with the whole feminine carload.

+++

There were 15 cars lining the sides of the highway at the Quarter, parked well behind the 2 racers. Everyone moved fast, to try to beat any oncoming traffic. Steve Arnholder and his date Laurie were running down the middle of the road, lit up by the cars' headlights, toward the marked end of the quarter to judge the winner. Laurie waved a tie-dyed bandana.

Joey, newly emboldened by the girls in Eileen's car, volunteered to wave the start, envisioning the tower of lights at a racetrack.

Dan leaned back on his Pontiac, shaking his head at his friend's antics. The dude was girl crazy. He thought maybe Joey should hang out with Eileen's crew.

The drivers sat working clutches, revving on the marked starting line, serious faces and clenched jaws as though this was a fight to the finish, an old-fashioned race for pinks. Tony's car held only himself and Maria, the passengers had left to stand with the other observers.

Riff had no passenger, causing Tony to entertain a quick thought as to whether the extra weight of a passenger could make the difference. But he was also proud of his old lady for wanting to stay.

Maria was inwardly freaking out. Why didn't she just get out? It's not like Tony would mind; he was all up in his groove. She was normally too chicken to even do a Chinese Fire Drill, for pity's sake. This was much heavier. But exciting too. She felt … pretty. And bold. She fantasized being the subject of a local teenage legend ………

At the finish line, Steve waved his go-ahead to starter Joey who called out to the drivers, "GENTLEMEN ... ready to rumble?"

Both engines revved in answer. As Joey lowered the bandana, the shrieking roar became deafening.

The crowd cheered, the girls jumping up and down, boys punching the air. The start line, now empty, filled with racing fans as they merged from both shoulders to follow the cars.

Maria held a guttural scream for the entire 13 seconds of the race. She was hoarse for the rest of the evening.

Riff's Mustang laid more rubber at the take-off, but there had been some slight fishtailing, unlike the straight line of Tony's tracks. Riff drove distracted, he knew he would see those rat-fink curved black lines in his dreams.

Tony basically emptied his mind of anything that did not push him forward. The finish line was like a magnet, the accelerator obeying his pressure. Only glimpsing the waving bandana, he was euphoric, though his legs almost betrayed him as he stepped out to receive his winner's acclaim. He covered by going slapstick to bestow a loud kiss on the Charger's hood. Only Maria, in a tight embrace, could feel his trembling.

Approaching from the south, a car's headlights scattered the crowd. Steve thought to wave the driver through, but the driver recognized Steve and asked what was going on. Steve quickly caught him up, complete with dramatic sound effects and gestures. Laurie twirled excitedly, the rainbow bandana her prop.

+++

Maria's dream that she and Tony become a local teen legend lasted for about a week and a half. A couple of new guys soon arrived in town. Bob drove a fast '55 Chevy 210. John drove a distinctive, canary yellow, '32 Ford coup. New hot wheels of the summer of '69, the stuff of legends.

😎 ☮ 😎

## Crispie Treat

*My sister and I benefited from having our grade school only a few blocks from both our dad's downtown business and the site of after-school Girl Scout meetings.*

Lynn shifted the load of books into the other arm and used her free right arm to re-position her purse on her shoulder. She looked up just in time to see her sister Kate as she was saying after-school toodles to her friends Susan and Marian. *Toodles* was Kate's newest favorite expression. Lynn thought her little sister should definitely take foreign languages when she got into high school. She had always created words, names, sound effects and even languages when they were at play. Lynn marveled at the girl's creativity.

"Ready Freddy?" asked Kate. She didn't stop but kept walking past her sister on the sidewalk.

Lynn fell into step and the two walked toward downtown from St. Joseph School. "So much homework," lamented Lynn as she shifted again the weight of her schoolbooks.

"Sorry Charlie. *We* got off easy. Miss Freyaldenhoven didn't feel good today so she forgot to give us any," answered Kate. "I just have to finish up the book report she gave us last week. So, what's up today at Girl Scouts?"

"Can't remember … it's been 3 weeks since last meeting," Lynn said while once again contorting to try to get the books in some shape to carry for several more blocks. "Here, Miss No Homework. Take a couple of these …." Just in front of the post office steps, she dropped the whole stack, stomped her foot and exhaled, her bangs wafting upwards, a familiar sight to Kate.

"Wasn't it something about the cooking badge?" Kate said to the sidewalk while bending to help with the books. "Lynn, have you ever heard of *Study Hall*? Couldn't you have cleared some of these books already? We should leave them at Dad's shop while we go to Girl Scouts."

Arriving at Simon's Grocery, Kate was telling the story of her classmate Gary's antics at recess. An odd child, apparently that day he was a lion "from China" and roared in each face he passed on the playground. Ceely Donahue had meowed back in his face, crushing the charade and causing Teddy to convert into an airplane.

The girls were all the way into the bakery section before the story ended, Lynn laughing at the imagined scenes playing in her head. Gary's older sister Diane was a classmate so she was familiar with the little brother's off-beat antics. Diane always referred to him as Goober Gary.

Crispies in a white paper sack – the girls' favorite weekly bakery snack that resembled a baked, cinnamony pie crust – were paid for at the front before they exited the store.

On the corner of Front and Oak, Lynn noticed frogs – *hoppy toads* in Sandy's world – jumping from a huge planter outside Greeson's Drug Store. The three frogs seemed in a race to get around the corner and hop into yet another planter. Silently waiting for the red light while munching their sweet pastry and watching cars go over the railroad tracks, Lynn and Kate saw Stan Tolliman's ancient, almost colorless pick-up truck loudly rattle by. Once, Lynn had commented that she didn't know what was holding that old thing together. Their dad had responded, "Now, Lynnie, that's not a nice way to talk about a guy who can't help his age." He was always cracking lame jokes like that.

At the TV repair shop the girls dropped their books on a countertop in the back, spoke to Miss Henry the secretary and flew out the door, having learned that their dad was out on a service call.

"Whew, that's better," Lynn said as she exercised her now empty arms.

Down the block, they passed Ollie Hammet outside his grocery store, sweeping the sidewalk, creating a small dust cloud. He greeted the girls and motioned for them to keep a wide berth. Kate tried to stifle a cough but couldn't.

The courthouse always caused Lynn and Kate to ominously pick up their pace; they regularly had to get shots for school inside the Health Department on the $2^{nd}$ floor. The old building's worn steps, white tile flooring, and tall ceilings with languid ceiling fans were features that foretold fear and pain in their imaginations. Shots were the worst things they'd ever experienced and every single incident was cause for drama sufficient to win an Academy Award.

Robinson Street's rows of dignified homes were always fodder for concocted stories of just what kind of families could afford to live in such large "mansions." More than one fantasy was spun and populated during their weekly walks. Sometimes there were kings and queens residing; often there were romantic balcony scenes, ala Romeo and Juliet.

A block from the First Baptist Church, where their troop would meet in the basement, a passing car revealed a little girl's hand holding a girl scout beanie waving at them from the back seat. Anna was going to beat them to the meeting.

Going down the basement stairs at the back of the church building, Lynn squinched up her nose at the familiar musty smell before moving into the small room that held Troop 491.

😎☮😎

# Burgers and Boyfriends

*Dedicated to ye olde (late 1960's) short order cooks/waitresses/crafters of burgers.
Though I <u>was</u> one such worker in high school, this story is fictional.*


Pauline and Judy each arrived at Bob & Herb's Drive-In at the same time, prompt for their 4-11pm shift. Judy was substituting for an under-the-weather Carla and had had to cancel a date. Pauline had been on the schedule for that Saturday night but would just as soon not be here in her tacky white-nylon-old-lady waitress uniform. But at least her ponytailed coif eliminated the perfectly awful hair net. Tonight's shift and Sunday morning opening were the least coveted work times among the employees who, for the most part, rated social activities a higher score than spending money. The *back-to-back* –

closing and then opening the next morning – was universally dreaded but at least there was Friday or Sunday evening for dates or family stuff.

Patsy and Margie gratefully handed over the reigns to their relief coworkers and, with the newfound energy miraculously found at the end of a shift, sprinted out through the back door after filling out time cards. Pauline took a large order right away and headed into the kitchen to fry three burgers and a chicken basket. Judy stayed up front when regulars Donnie and Fred Ray came into the tiny dining area.

"Hey guys," she said. "Let me know when you want to order."

Donnie responded with silence and a two-finger wave. Fred Ray said, "Yup," and went to the jukebox, assuming the position of studying the song titles, both hands slapping the glass to whatever tune was already in his head. Two quarters would buy six songs. A decision worthy of one's full attention, hungry or not.

Judy wandered to the back. When the first notes of *Duke of Earl* sounded, Pauline remarked knowingly, "Fred Ray's here. What'll he play if they ever change out that record?" She methodically dressed three burger buns rowed up on the scarred butcher-block counter, moving back and forth between the grill and the chilled tray of prepped vegetable toppings. Judy took over at the deep fryer, watching the chicken and fries while letting her mind wander.

Pauline asked, "Was Billy mad when you had to cancel tonight?"

"Yeah, but he got over it. He's taking me home later," Judy replied lethargically. "Don't say anything, but I'm kinda thinking of breaking up with him."

Pauline looked at her friend like she'd spoken in Portuguese or something. "For real? Why? He's soooo cute. Wait, don't start until I get this order out."

A bit of an early supper rush kept the announcement unexamined for another thirty minutes. Dewayne Harlis drove up and ordered his usual – two Frito Chili Pies and a 25 cent cherry Coke for himself, and three hamburger patties for his dog, Rascal. Dewayne sat in his truck while Sam Harwell stood leaning on his Mustang convertible, smoking and talking to Dewayne. Sam was teasing Rascal, trying to get him to bark.

After Judy had made two milkshakes and a hot fudge sundae for a family in a station wagon,

Pauline motioned her into the back, out of earshot of Fred Ray, Donnie, and the sound of their continuing tunes. "Well?" Pauline asked.

"Oh, I don't know," Judy responded through a sigh. She twisted a plastic straw around her left index finger. "It's really not anything specific. It's not like he's done anything horrible. I just don't feel the same way about him as I did last year. I used to think we'd get married, have three kids, a nice house out on Lake Beaverfork, or maybe in West Gate, live happily ever after. But now I can't see myself with him even as far out as next month. Shouldn't that mean it's over?"

"Judy Judy Judy!" Pauline scolded. "What about prom? What about senior trip? And senior play?"

"Well, now you see my problem with timing," whined Judy. "Should I go ahead and break up with him now, which would probably mean *I would* have more fun the last two months of high school but then *he would* be miserable. Or, hang in there and be sensitive to his feelings and put my own aside. I'll tell ya, you're lucky you don't have a steady. It's not always groovy, ya know."

Pauline decided to ignore her coworker's thoughtlessly conceited final remark. Judy could be so insensitive sometimes; she seemed to be hopelessly dense about other people's feelings. Once, Judy had asked Pauline to cover her Saturday night shift at work because Billy didn't want to be alone after the basketball team had lost the regional tournament. An unwritten rule, covering on a Saturday was for a really big reason, maybe illness or family events. "My boyfriend's sad" didn't really cut it. And even if that was the actual, real reason, most girls would have the sensitivity to tell a better story.

"Well, you're *sure* that Billy would be all torn up about it?" Pauline asked, her mental trip down memory lane summoning her inner mean girl. She studied the nails on her right hand.

A knock on the front window sent each girl into reflexive motion. Both scooted to the front where Pauline opened the sliding window to wait on Tina, another part-time employee.

"Pauline, my bestest pal, ol' buddy, would you go back to the office and get my paycheck? If I even race through there I'll smell like a cheeseburger the rest of the niiiiiiight," Tina pleaded dramatically.

"Oh you poor baby," Pauline said. She walked back to retrieve the enveloped paycheck and then held it just out of Tina's reach. "Now Tina, I checked, and since this paycheck does, *itself,* have a powerful aroma of Eau de Cheeseburger, maybe you'd rather just let me keep it? I got nothing against funky money."

Tina stretched her perfectly made-up face into a grimaced response. "You're as funny as a rubber crutch. Now gimme."

Pauline was forced to end the game and hand the envelope over when three cars pulled into the parking lot. "Don't spend it all in one place, girl," she advised her friend's rapidly retreating back.

Donnie and Fred Ray decided they were ready to eat and added their order to the others. Pauline and Judy prepared and served several meals and then replenished the vanilla soft serve mix before opening another carton of black walnut ice cream. Pauline wiped down counters while waiting for Judy to revisit the subject of her impending breakup. But Judy was not forthcoming, seeming to grow a bit introspective.

Donnie and Fred Ray finally left the dining area, but only after their last song played –

*Runaway*. Pauline opined that they would probably go drive the circle about a thousand times. By evening's end she knew she'd been right. Bob & Herb's was the southernmost turnaround on the circle, and she'd noticed Donnie's red Impala several times among the other vehicles, making a well-practiced maneuver through the lot and back out onto Harkrider to leisurely repeat the downtown loop.

A mutual friend of Judy and Pauline's pulled up with her date. Trudy and Scott came inside and split an order of fries. Judy fixed their order by rote. One cherry vanilla Dr. Pepper and a large suicide to go with the fries. Trudy gave the girls a litany of who they'd seen in town that evening, who'd been hangin' at Dog 'n Suds down the street, who'd been at the Conway Theater, whose cars had been at the skating rink as well as a rumor they'd heard about Daniel Fortenberry. Reportedly, he had a date that night with an older girl – a freshman at ASTC.

"Well, la de da, but how'd Daniel Fortenberry swing that?" was Judy's opinion that received only shrugs in reply.

When Trudy and Scott said good-bye on their way out, Judy said, "Don't do anything I wouldn't do!"

Trudy stuck out her tongue at her friend and followed her boyfriend to his car, a Barracuda that was the envy of all Scott's friends. His father had awarded the teenager with the car after Scott kept his end of a bargain to make good grades.

Judy seemed to remain in the withdrawn funk she'd plunked herself into after telling Pauline about breaking off with Billy.

Pauline thought that she would wait for the girl to continue the discussion, rather than prod her into it. She found she actually couldn't gather up much emotion or opinion about whichever way Judy would or should choose, she was mostly just curious, or more like *nosy* as her mom would say. And Judy had been correct, if kinda mean, in summing up Pauline's current single status ... she'd never been in a serious relationship before and found it hard to sympathize with someone who was mostly a work buddy, not a close friend or classmate. But the whole mood was bringing her down a little and she was feeling her single status as a bigger lack than it had been before Judy rudely pointed it out. So, which was more of a bummer … being single or headed to splitsville?

Checking the clock to note one more hour before closing, Pauline shook off the self-pity she'd summoned, telling herself that there was no answer. She told Judy that she would make up some hamburger patties for the next day.

Judy merely waved at her from her perch, leaning on the front counter and staring out at the traffic on Harkrider Street.

After fifteen minutes, Pauline had pushed out the doldrums and moved on to making a plan to close the restaurant, a process that they could start soon. She heard the front door open. Judy's Billy came in and pulled out a chair. Pauline sang under her breath, "My boyfriend's back and you're gonna be in trouble …." She backed into the kitchen area after seeing it was Billy. Judy had not said anything; Billy was silent too.

Billy got out his wallet and studied the insides, ran his pocket comb through his hair, whistled the tune of a Pepsodent TV commercial, and retied his shoes before saying, "Um, hey Judy, um … been busy tonight?"

Judy sauntered back over to where she could see him around the ice cream machine. "Yeah. Kinda. So, where you been?"

"Around ... nowhere, ya know. You gonna get off on time?"

Judy glanced up at the clock and answered, "Yeah, like usual, around 11. Why?"

"Um, uh, I got some stuff I wanna talk about and I know your curfew is 12."

Judy swallowed hard; a thousand thoughts ran through her head. Since Billy seemed as sullen as he was when she talked to him earlier that day, and he would hardly look at her, whatever was on his mind was likely not a happy surprise. "Oh, okay, yeah, uh, can you give me a hint?"

"Well, uh, only if you wanna do this now instead of later," he told the floor.

"Hold on, I'll be right back."

Judy scanned the parking lot before heading to the back to talk to Pauline. Whispering, she hastily asked her coworker if there was any way it would be okay for her to leave 20 minutes early if she did half the closing chores real quick.

Pauline looked up while scraping the grease from the hamburger grill into its trap, "Is something wrong?"

"No ... well, yeah, I think maybe there is. Billy wants to talk. That never happens. Pretty please? I'll make it up to you, even work a shift if you want."

Judy returned to the snarky mood that she'd developed when Pauline had been so dismissive earlier. Though she didn't mind closing alone, she said, "You can't wait a half hour to break his heart?"

Judy put her finger to her lips and glanced in the direction of Billy's position out front. "See, the thing is, I had kinda talked myself out of the whole thing, and now, here he is with something on his mind. Please?"

"Oh. Of course. Go on, I'll close up," Pauline rolled her eyes and waved her friend off. "Hmm, I'm gettin' gladder all the time that I don't have such troubles, after all. Go. Good luck."

Judy took care of her time card, grabbed her purse and ran out, blowing kisses to Pauline on the way.

Pauline saw that there were no more cars on the lot except Billy's and returned to her chores. As she swept the floors she planned the order in which she'd get everything else done. The ice cream machine would need to be broken down and cleaned last but she could wash all the other dishes when she finished sweeping and mopping. Then she'd need to pick up trash out on the parking lot and get the cash drawers emptied and stowed in the locked hidey hole in the office. Sometimes Herb came to get it at closing time but other times, he wanted it put away safely. Tonight he'd left a note that he would not be coming in.

Pauline was filling the mop bucket with hot water when she heard the door open and slam shut. The swinging gate into the service area creaked so she turned off the water and dried her hands as she noticed Billy's tail lights leaving the lot. Judy suddenly appeared at the sink, her face red, and she was breathing hard.

"What ... what happened? Where's he going?" Pauline managed to stutter.

That brought on the tears that Judy had apparently held at bay.

Pauline was frozen until she thought to grab a napkin to offer her friend. "Judy?"

"He broke up with me," she said through broken sobs. "Do you even believe that?"

"He ... oh wow," Pauline answered. "Just wow."

They heard a car door slam so Pauline scooted around a wilting Judy to wait on the customer. But she was back in only a minute. "Just someone switching drivers. It's okay."

Judy was slowly emptying, but still mopping her face. "I was right to want to end things with him, but he beat me to it and now it's my turn to cry."

Pauline's mind raced to try to understand why, if this result would have occurred anyway, that her friend was so seemingly distraught. She deemed herself truly without a clue about relationships.

Judy continued, "I know, I know, I'm a mess for something that I was gonna do anyway. Dumb."

Pauline heard that as permission to proceed. "Well, okay, do you want to say why he did it?"

"Long story short, he STARTED out saying he felt like I didn't love him anymore and that he thought we should break up so I could move on," Judy's tears had stopped and now she had her hand on her hip, all attitude. "But I smelled a rat and said 'Billy, don't be a hero. Tell me what's really going on.' And then he started in that he was considering joining the army and that might mean he'd have to go to 'Nam and he could get shot or something, and before all that happened ... get this ... he thought he might like to date Brenda Shuster."

Pauline's hands flew to her mouth, and if she were forced to admit it, mostly to hide the mean grin that she honestly hadn't intended to pop out instead of shock and sympathy. To try to recover, she remained silent.

Judy balled up the destroyed napkin and threw it at the wall over the sinks. "I mean, I didn't want to stay with him, but I wanted him to *want* me to stay with him, ya know? And then come to find that he doesn't want me at all, he wants *Brenda Shuster*." Brenda's name came out like Judy was chewing glass as she said it, but there were no more tears.

Pauline recovered and put both hands on Judy's shoulders. "I'm so sorry. I don't ... it sounds like Billy wants to be a fool with his life, and you'll be better off without him." And then, mocking the gravelly tone Judy had used, she said, "He's *Brenda Shuster's* problem now."

Judy laughed out loud, longer than the rescue joke deserved, stomped her right foot and then squared her shoulders. "Yeah, that's right. What's love got to do with it anyway? I'm a free agent now. Let's get this place closed down, huh?"

😎 ☮ 😎

## Debbie Fowler's Books:

**Out of Print:**
> The Boomers' Next Frontier
> Empty Nest, Full Hookups

Available:

> '62 Chevy, an Auto-Biography
> The FloraDoras Meet the Cosmic Catfish
> A Jasper Tale


**The Adventures of The Wilmas (series)**
> Objects in Life are Closer Than They Appear
> Looking Out My Back Door
> Great Pretenders

Made in the USA
Monee, IL
25 August 2025